Book
1/15/22

By Tom Brewster

Beacon Publishing Group

ISBN (Paperback): 9781961504172

Book 1/15/22

Cover Design by Jerry Parsons
Exterior Design by Lori Pace
Edited by Gerard Hernandez

Beacon Publishing Group, New York, NY 10001
www.beaconpublishinggroup.com

Manufactured in the United States of America

This book is dedicated To All United States Military Men and Women Who Have Served to Protect Our Country

Chapter One

Casey was sitting in his little boat office. A flickering light from a kerosene heater danced against the drab green walls. The November wind had iced over the windows, but the lake was still visible through the glaze. Sail boats in the slip bobbed in the water, the sky a dismal gray stretched on forever. There was a sensation in his stomach, a fluttering that he loved and hated at the same time. It couldn't be explained. It was a will-o- the wisp sensation crawling on his skin and occupying his mind. It was the phantom scent and flash of memories churning in his mind.

He didn't live in the past, but the past was closing in on him. The things he had done would qualify as a bestseller in a fiction novel. Things he needed to keep under wraps. They were dangerous but somehow seemed mundane when they happened but looking back, they were extraordinary. He was a complicated man living a complicated life.

Two agents from the FBI would be showing up in a few moments. Special Agent Ford had called him on Friday evening stating that he and Agent Tyrese Green would be there to ask questions on Monday. Casey patiently informed Agent Ford that he had answered all the questions he intended to answer. "You guys have been bugging me for twenty-five years. Why don't you just fuck off?" He had said.

Ford replied, "We'll be there. You can answer or take the Fifth. It's up to you."

Now as Casey reflected on his life; the fluttering was filling him to the brim. He wasn't sure if this was reality or a strange, extraordinary dream.

Chapter Two

Fog hanging in the trees had settled on the ground creating a slick invisible frosting. A black - 2019 Chevy sedan meandering into the lane in slow motion went into a slide nearly taking route into a ditch. After coming to a stop two men got out of the car and gingerly navigated the cobblestone walkway towards the office. They were both wearing blue windbreakers, white shirts, and red ties. Both young and athletic. One of them black, the other white. Casey surmised the black guy was Tyrese Green. The other, Agent Ford.

There had been a gradual evolution over time that changed the makeup of his antagonist. Back in the day when the FBI started looking at him the agents were all middle-aged white guys. Now teams of men and women, blacks and whites and on at least one occasion an all-black team had come to interrogate him. A white agent with a black partner was routine these days.

Casey crossed the room and looked at himself in the mirror. A navy-blue 'life is good' baseball cap covered his thick gray hair. All but one small brown patch in his beard below his lip was the only remnant of original hair color. Even his full bushy eyebrows were as white as snow. He didn't look a thing like the guy the FBI was looking for back in the nineties. Sometimes changes are a good thing.

After three quick knocks at the office door, a shout, "FBI!" Casey opened the door. "What's your hurry, boys? You've had thirty years to nab me. Do you think

I'm gonna run now?" Casey said.

The white guy held his badge at eye level. "You already identified yourself on the phone. I don't need to see your identification, Special Agent Lee Ford." Casey said. He looked at the black agent. "How you doing, Tyrese?" emphasizing the first part of his name, sounding as much like Jethro Bodine as possible. Casey didn't have a racist bone in his body, but he wanted to hit where it hurt.

Agent Green frowned, a quiet "humph" escaped his lips.

"You can stop with the redneck dialogue, Casey, I've read your file. I know you're a smart sonofabitch," Ford said.

Casey walked over to his desk and picked up the copy of the police sketch that appeared in magazines every few years, and now it was posted on the web in articles that were still circulating thirty years after the first time it appeared in the Boston Globe.

"Take a seat," Casey said, handing the picture to Ford.

Both agents pulled up folding metal chairs. "Nice place," Tyrese said, scanning the dismal surroundings. The cold air was already seeping through his clothing, the metal chair frigid.

Agent Ford glanced at the sketch and placed it on Casey's desk. He had seen it a thousand times. He was in college the first time, and that was the tenth anniversary of its printing.

"That guy doesn't look much like me," Casey said.

Ford picked it up, looking at it with a casual smile. "You have some jowls, but the shape of your face is similar. Behind that beard it's probably remarkably similar," he said.

"How about the eyebrows? These babies I have are something to be proud of. I'd be ashamed to walk around with bijou thickets like that over my eyes."

"I don't know about that. My grandmother had eyebrows like a sasquatch, but with a tweezers and a little honing them, they were pencil thin," Ford said, again the corners of his mouth turning up slightly. He looked amused, but he was serious. He believed he might be talking to one of the perpetrators of the most infamous unsolved crimes in American history. He wanted to prove it, and put him away for a long time, but he had a little latent admiration for Casey too.

"Are you going to read me my rights," Casey said.

"No, that's not necessary. Unless you want to confess."

"Sure. You got me. I'm DB Cooper," Casey said facetiously.

Ford smiled. "He got two hundred thousand; nothing to laugh at fifty years ago, but you copped five hundred million," Ford said. Casey smiled, suppressing a little pride. Ford focused on Casey's lying eyes. You did it, you sonofabitch, he thought.

"Are you referring to that Ida Swigert Graham Museum heist?" Casey said.

"We're not the first agents to suggest that, are we?" Tyrese Green said. Casey smiled that vague little smile again. "Wasn't that a couple of Boston cops who did that job?" he asked, pretending to be serious. He cocked his head to one side and furrowed the lines on his forehead. "I used a little of the proceeds to decorate the office," he said, opening his hand in a fanning motion.

Agent Ford interrupted. "Nobody knew why Boston PD kept running that sketch in the papers. They just asked the public for information. When the Bureau ran it nationally there were at least five people who made you in that sketch," he said, tapping the sketch with his index finger.

"Really? Eyebrows and all?"

"Yep."

"You know I've heard that before, Agent Ford. It's in my file, right? How many times have I been questioned about this crap? I was in Boston that week. That's already been established. You guys always want to know what I was doing. Do you remember what you were doing thirty years ago? Some people think I look like this sketch. Maybe I do but there's only so many faces in the world to go around. Lots of guys probably look like that sketch."

The Ida Swigert Graham Museum heist was the number one unsolved crime in Bureau history. DB Cooper was a legend, but the ISG caper was higher on the Bureau's list, but It seemed almost amateurish in how it went down. The museum was being run by an amateur security manager, and the security system was completely inadequate for the treasures that were on display there. Motion detectors were throughout the entire building, but they were unsophisticated and outdated. A silent alarm at the guard station was routed straight to the police station, but a button had to be depressed in order to activate it. The motion detectors merely alerted the security desk of movement within the museum, but it didn't alert the cops. Two inexperienced armed guards were manning the security desk. By modern standards, the security system was a joke. Still, the heist was so simple it was hard to believe it succeeded.

On March 15th, 1990, two men dressed in police uniforms showed up at the side door at about 1:30 am and hit the buzzer at the employee entrance. One guard was making his rounds at the time, and the other was at the security desk. The men looked like authentic police officers on the closed circuit tv, so they were buzzed in. They said they were investigating a disturbance and needed to speak to the guards. Once they were inside one of the men told the guard they had a warrant for his arrest. They ordered him to step out from behind the guard desk and present identification. He complied. They handcuffed him and then politely told him they were there to rob the place. He was out of position to activate the silent alarm. When the other guard returned from his rounds, he was handcuffed, and they were taken to the basement. Their eyes were wrapped with duck-tape, and they were strapped to a pole. From the data retrieved from the motion detectors and video it was revealed they were there for almost an hour. Twelve paintings and an ancient Roman galea were removed. The total worth was five hundred million. The men disappeared into the night, never to be seen again.

Agent Ford picked up the police sketch and scrutinized it. "Yep, the shape of your eyes, your chin, forehead, hairline. It's all very similar, even now at your age. You know we've overlain this with photographs of you, and it's remarkable how well it matches up."

"It's a drawing, Agent Ford. You could just change the lines, lengthen the face, scroll back the hairline.

You could make it an exact match, couldn't you. The problem is, it's still a sketch," Casey said.

Ford placed the sketch back on Casey's desk. "It was five years before we started looking at you, but we took down a crooked art dealer in Charleston who tried to cut a deal with the District Attorney. That's when we started thinking maybe it was you. He told us a guy tried to unload a Rembrandt from the ISG theft, but it was too hot to touch. Funny part was that he identified the guy in this sketch as the guy who approached him with that painting. You look a lot like that sketch, man."

"It's still a sketch, and it's not me," Casey said.

Casey had seen that sketch at least fifty times in newspapers, and on tv. Now occasionally it popped up on the web. He had never asked how the sketch was relevant to the robbery. It was definitely not one of the police imposters. None of the interrogators were willing to give up information about it. He didn't know how much they knew. It was a matter of holding back information that only the guilty would know. Casey was careful not to ask too many questions. He was surprised that Ford was talkative today. They usually just asked question with stone-faced expressions and avoided conversation. Casey liked Ford better than other agents who were there before him, but he knew that Ford and Green were there to take him down if they could.

"We've got a few sources that put you in Charleston back then. Do you mind telling me what you were doing there?"

"You said that was thirty years ago?"

"Twenty-five."

"I was all over the place in those days. I don't know

what I was doing in Charleston. Like I said before. Do you remember what you were doing twenty-five years ago?"

"I was in elementary school."

"Time flies," Casey said.

"Casey, do you know the name, Jake Brenner?"

Casey stared passively at Ford, careful not to show emotion. Yes, he knew Jake Brenner. The wheels inside Casey's head were turning. Ford knew something, but Casey didn't know where he was going with this. Was Ford connecting the dots?

"Not that I remember," Casey lied.

"How about Terry Smith? Does that name mean anything to you, Casey," Ford asked.

Casey hesitated for a long moment. "I vaguely remember Terry," he said.

Chapter Three

Casey was nineteen years old in 1966. There was a war going on in Viet Nam. He was like most young men his age. He wouldn't be able to find Viet Nam on the map, but it would soon change his life. From the time he was seventeen Casey was a drifter moving from one small town to another without the slightest notion of what his future might bring. Living in a single one room apartment without television for entertainment and being broke most of the time, Casey became an avid reader. He bought his books at Goodwill Stores or yard sales. He read math, history, science, anything he could get his hands on. He would be considered well read by any standard, but he didn't have access to current events. He was very intelligent, but he really didn't know what was going on in the world.

Being smart didn't mean he was working a high paying job. In fact, it was just the opposite. He was working in an auction sale barn in Hopedale, Illinois. Horses, cattle, and hogs were auctioned each Monday, beginning at 10:00 am and ending when all animals were sold. Casey's job was herding the entire menagerie one critter at a time into the ring, keeping them under control as a fat guy in a flannel shirt and safari hat rattled off the bids over a loudspeaker. It didn't matter how quickly the purchases were affected, those future hamburgers, and pork chops managed to relieve themselves in the ring. When all sales were completed, it was Casey's job to clean things up. Tuesday through Sunday, feeding animals and shoveling straw saturated with urine and feces from the stalls kept him busy.

Casey was living in a room above the poolhall in Delavan, Illinois, so he was having his mail delivered to the auction barn. After a long Monday night shooing animals into and out of the sales ring, Mr. Rogie, the auctioneer, walked slowly into the stall where Casey was knee deep in cow manure. He handed an envelope to Casey and said, "Good luck, kid. Have a good life."

Casey opened the envelope to find a letter from Uncle Sam welcoming him into the US Army. At that point he was on a route that would cross paths with Jake Brenner and Terry Smith, and eventually to that conversation with Special Agents Ford and Green. Going into the service wasn't exactly a career path but it didn't matter. At that point in his life, he was like a marble on a warped floor, rolling around until he was stranded in a slump where he remained until an unexpected kick started him rolling again. Getting his draft notice was just another thing to push him into another unknown direction.

Casey was drunk for two days before he had to report to the post office in Washington, Illinois where a military bus would round up the draftees and transport them to the train station in Chicago. When his girlfriend (a senior in high school,) learned he was off to see the wizard she promptly dumped him. He was ticked off and broken hearted, but he could understand why she wouldn't wait two years for him to come back home and resume his career in scooping shit out of animal stalls. Still, it set him off on a rampage. He had two fist fights with total strangers and punched a guy he knew for wishing him well on his departure. Most people liked Casey, but for those two days he was a sonofabitch nobody would have any affection for.

Most small towns in central Illinois where Casey had hung his hat were no bigger than two thousand people. They all looked the same. They had a main street restaurant, a pool hall, grocery store, and a library. It was a mystery even to himself why he would find one of them more attractive than the other. He moved so often that if he had set sail for Los Angeles or New York he would have spent less time on the road. The largest city he had ever seen was Peoria, Illinois, and that was just a drive through.

The bus ride through Chicago gave Casey a new perspective of the world. The lights, the skyscrapers, and a lake so deep and wide it seemed to go on forever. Inside the train station the diesel fumes mingled with the smell of hot steel and oil from the train engines. Casey's eyes wandered taking in everything. The arching ceiling was smudged with smoke residue. It was like a dark dreary cave and higher than any building in Delavan. It was big enough to enclose the entire town. Forty draftees lined up on the concrete median between incoming and outgoing trains where they waited to board a passenger car. A sergeant dressed in green fatigues, starched and rigidly pressed with creases as sharp as a knife, barked orders and strutted around with confidence that came with unbridled authority. A thin, fair skinned young man next to Casey with a concerned expression, staring across the vast enclosure. His arms were pressed tight against his side and his hands were trembling like a man about to walk into a gas chamber. He glanced nervously at Casey several times. He wanted to say something, but he just stood there with his mouth formed to make a statement; his words stuck in his throat. Casey smiled. "I guess we're in the Army now," he said.

"Yes, we are. We're in the Army now," he groaned.

"Is this your first time in Chicago?" Casey asked.

The guy stood there, still rigid, but his hands had stopped shaking. "No, but this stuff is worrying me, I don't want to kill anybody, and I don't want to die," he said.

It was the first time Casey thought about fighting and dying. Up until now it was just a process he had to go through. Signing up for the draft had been a nuisance, and the all-day physical exam was a hassle he had to endure. He didn't think about where he was being routed. Now here he was, heading off into a place where he thought he would never be. The guy next to him was scared but Casey was just annoyed at losing his freedom.

"I'm Jake Brenner," the guy said meekly.

"Casey Rakestraw."

Obviously, Jake Brenner didn't have the same attitude about their situation as Casey had. As the train left the station Brenner was sticking with Casey like glue. They couldn't have been more different. Jake was a timid fearful kid, and Casey, independent and rugged. Casey was six feet tall, 185 pounds with dark hair and dark eyes. A three-day beard made him look as tough as leather. Brenner's fair skin, blond hair and blue eyes made him look younger than he was. He carried himself like a pre-school teacher, or a florist. When they boarded the train Brenner followed Casey into a sleeper car where they joined four others. They were bound for Fort Campbell, Kentucky.

Chapter Four

The sun was sinking behind gray clouds beyond the barren trees along the lake. Casey thought about Jake Brenner from that initial meeting between them fifty-four years ago. "Old Shakey Jake Brenner, now I remember" he said aloud. Tyrese Green adjusted his weight in his chair anticipating Casey's remarks. Casey crossed his arms and leaned back in his chair.

"Why don't you tell me about old Shakey Jake Brenner," Special Agent Ford said.

Casey glanced out the window, "It looks like it might snow," he said.

"Casey, we're not here to talk about the weather. Why don't you tell us what you know about Brenner?"

"I suppose you already know everything there is to know about him. Why don't you tell me what you guys know about Shakey Jake?" Casey said.

"We know you were buds in Nam," Agent Green said.

"I was in basic training with him, and I saw him once in Vietnam. That doesn't make us buds, Tyrese," Casey said, again using his phony southern drawl. "What else you got? You probably know him better than I do," he added.

"He was in Boston the week of the heist, just like you were," Agent Ford said.

Casey picked up the sketch from his desk. "This doesn't look like Jake Brenner," he said.

"He could fit the description of the two police

impersonators," Green interjected.

Casey snorted softly. "That's not what I heard. I've read about this case. Those two security guards didn't remember anything about those guys. If they did, where's the sketch that looks like Shakey Jake?" Now Casey had been given a dose of confidence. If they knew anything at all about Brenner, they would have known he had less guts than the Cowardly Lion in the Wizard of Oz. He wouldn't have the nerve to steal a piece of gum in a candy shop. They're on a fishing trip, Casey thought.

Lee Ford scooted his chair back and got up. He strolled to the window and looked out. "It does look like it might snow," he said. He put both hands in his pockets. "Has anybody ever told you where that sketch came from, Casey? You've never asked. You just said the guards at the museum didn't have a clue. You've seen it in the paper, and on tv. We've been careful not to let the public know how this guy fits in."

Casey shrugged. "So?"

"I'm curious. Your file shows you've been asked about it several times. Not once have you asked about the sketch. You have never asked, what does this man have to do with the heist. Never, not even once."

"So, I'm not a curious person," Casey said.

Casey already knew and Ford knew how he knew it. Casey's gut tightened slightly. Agent Ford studied Casey's expression. FBI Agents were trained to see a lie on someone's face and in their eyes. Did he look down and to the left? Did he fold his arms across his chest? Was there strain around his nose and lips? These were all signs they looked for, but Casey didn't care. A confession had to come from his lips or be written with a pen. He didn't care how many traits were surfacing, he knew they wouldn't stand up in court as evidence or be admissible in testimony. It was irrelevant.

Fifty-four years ago, when he stepped off the train in Clarksville, Tennessee, he wouldn't have believed he would be here in his little boat shop on Lake Waubesa, Wisconsin, being interrogated by the FBI. It was a lifetime ago and a world away. He didn't believe he would ever be so important even as a malefactor, but here he was.

Casey's memory was fresh about being drafted, even after all this time. Personnel were lined up on the sidewalk after departing from the train. The temperature was fifty-four degrees when they left Grand Central Station in Chicago, but eighteen hours later in Clarksville, Tennessee, it was a muggy ninety-one. Jake Brenner was talkative, staying right on Casey's tail. He must have believed Casey would protect him somehow. "What do you think they're going to do to us?" he asked timidly. Casey laughed. "I don't think they want to hurt us. Don't they want us to fight a war? If they cripple or kill us, we won't be of much use, will we?" he said. Brenner giggled like a girl.

They were transported by bus to Fort Campbell, Kentucky. Four sergeants were sitting in the front two seats talking casually. The guys had loosened up a little. They were talking about sports, their families and girls they left behind. One of the sergeants looked over his shoulder and said, "You all don't need to worry about them girls. Jody already has her legs wrapped all up around him." Some laughed, and a few others booed. It didn't seem like the army Casey had heard about. It wasn't unpleasant, merely an inconvenience.

Casey's bus unloaded along with four others carrying forty passengers each. The draftees were lined up, taught how to salute and stand at attention. Every now and then a sergeant would tell them they were the sorriest looking bunch of girls he had ever welcomed into the army. They were issued military fatigues, enormous white boxer underwear, socks, and a duffle bag large enough to pack everything they needed. It weighed eighty pounds when filled. They were routed into a large metal building, lined up and relieved of their hair. What had been 160 long haired hippies now had heads like baby birds shining like a new dime. That was the induction process. When it was finished, they were marched into an auditorium and ordered to pick one of the hundreds of cots lined up in a row. Brenner was quick to grab one right next to Casey. When the lights went out, Casey thought, "This is easy."

At four am the lights came back on. The double steel doors banged open, the sound ringing off the walls like a bomb. Twenty drill sergeants rushed through the doors each holding a garbage can lid and a military baton. As the batons struck the metal lids the noise was like a freight train smashing through a metal building.

"Get outside! Get outside! Get outside," they shouted, their voices guttural and angry. Young men were falling from their cots, scrambling to their feet, disoriented and panicked. A sergeant standing next to Casey's bed struck his garbage can lid with such force it split away from the handle. "Get outside, you fuck'n maggots!"

Casey shoved his legs into his fatigues, sending

them down the same leg opening. As he was trying to readjust a sergeant charged him shouting. "We ain't got time to dress! Grab all your shit and get outside!" Casey zipped his fatigue zipper and grabbed his shoes and duffle bag. He didn't know where he was going but he set out in a dead run. He thought about the pigs and cattle he had routed into the auction barn, running and baying, and squealing. In a surreal moment he laughed. Jake Brenner was struggling to carry his duffle bag and boots. First the boots would fall, and while trying to pick them up, the duffle bag would roll off his shoulder and hit the ground. A drill sergeant charged at Brenner shouting, spit flying into the air. Nose to nose, he barked orders growling like a wild animal. Brenner's lips were quivering and hands shaking like an oak leaf in a breeze.

In those few moments, the entire area had been transformed into an outdoor insane asylum. White shiny bald heads were bobbing like ping pong balls, weaving and stampeding down a hill towards four buses idling in the road. In only minutes 160 newbies were standing in a formation breathing heavily, half-dressed and in their bare feet. Brenner had kicked one boot and then the other rolling them down the hill until he found his way to the formation. He found a space next to Casey. His feet were bleeding, his chest heaving like it might explode. Flashlight beams were crisscrossing in the dark as the craziness was reaching a fever pitch. Brenner saw the drill sergeant who had ripped him a new one was headed his way. His features were taut with fear as he grimaced trying to hold back tears. The other men were standing at attention as rigid as fence posts, and some of them were terrified, but

Brenner stuck out like a sore thumb. His nemesis, Sergeant Lloyd Lilly, shined his flashlight onto Brenner's face. Whatever self-control Brenner had was gone in the wind, and for some ungodly reason he grinned.

"What the fuck are you grinning at, boy! Are you fuck'n stupid? Do you think I'm your girlfriend, boy! Do you want to fuck me!" Sergeant Lilly snarled. The words came in such a practiced cadence it was obvious Brenner wasn't the first recipient of his rage.

Brenner was shaking from his head to his feet. He tried to answer, but instead he snorted, spewing spit into the air in a giggling fit.

"Goddamn It, boy, get down and give me twenty push-ups!" Sergeant Lilly roared.

Brenner started for the ground, but somewhere between standing at attention and the prone position he went limp, falling like a victim of a second-round knockout punch, face first into the gravel. A different sergeant came charging up. "Get up, soldier!" He squatted on his haunches and examined Brenner's face. Sergeant Lilly leaned down to look. "This boy is out, Lloyd, he's unconscious!" The little fuckers passed out!", he laughed. They looked at each other for a moment as if their might have been humor in the situation. Sergeant Lilly slapped the other sergeant on the shoulder. They both laughed again. After a quiet moment they got up and got back into the lunacy, shouting orders like madmen. Sergeant Lilly charged at Casey shouting and pointing at Brenner's duffle bag. Casey didn't understand a word, but he realized that he was supposed to pick up Brenner's equipment. He grabbed the duffle with one hand and tossed it onto his shoulder and ran for the bus. After he was seated, he looked out the window to see Sergeant Lilly softly slapping Brenner's face as he lie on the ground. Casey didn't see Brenner again until a year later in Vietnam.

Chapter Five

Agent Ford walked across the room, the floors creaking beneath his feet. He slid the chair closer to Casey's desk. "Why don't you use some of that ISG money to upgrade your facilities here, Casey?" he said.

"If I had some of it I would, but like I've said a hundred times, I didn't do it." He smiled sheepishly.

"I think you did, but that stuff is so hot you can't unload it," Agent Green said. He was playing second fiddle to Ford, but he wanted his presence known.

"You guys have a psychological file on me. You know me. I might have done it just for shits and grins." He hesitated for a moment, and then added, "but I didn't do it, did I?"

"What about Terry Smith? Tell us about Terry Smith."

Casey's eyes were focused on Ford's face, but his mind was somewhere else. He knew Terry. Denying it would be impossible. Terry Smith was a force of nature. He was a crazy sonofabitch, and it was a good thing for a lot of guys in country that he was. More guys were still breathing because of Terry than any other Huey pilot in Vietnam.

After finishing AIT in Panama, Casey and twenty other troops were bused to Miami where they caught a TWA flight to Oakland, California, and from there to Cam Ranh Bay, Vietnam. As the plane descended, Casey looked out the window, the sunlight cutting through the clouds rolling across the ground in waves.

Crystal clear water in the bay glittering near the beach became a deep and blue as it stretched away from the land. Without the army base a half mile from the water it might have been a tropical paradise. Casey wasn't thinking about war. He was in awe of all that had happened, how far away he was from the flat ground and cornfields of home. At that moment he thought Cam Ranh Bay was the most beautiful place on earth. As hours clicked away, he would find he was on the fringes of hell.

When they deplaned, the men he had traveled with were dispersed in every direction. Casey's orders were to report to headquarters for his assignment. An odd train of events happened at that time that would linger for the rest of Casey's life. In 1967 the war was accelerating at breakneck speed. There were so many troops arriving daily it was hard to get them to their designated combat post. The convoy Casey was supposed be with had headed north two hours before he arrived. When Casey entered Sergeant Beatty's office, there was an angry expression on the sergeant's face. "Private Rakestraw reporting for duty." Casey said.

Sergeant Beatty shuffled the papers on his desk, lined them up carefully, and then threw them into the air! "Goddamn it! You're two hours late," he shouted. Sergeant Beatty looked at him as if he might be a pile of cow manure. Finally, he exhaled to keep his head from blowing off his shoulders. Casey was still standing at attention. His boots pressed together at the heels, his thumbs aligned with the seams of his fatigues, his eyes focused straight ahead. "Relax, kid, you're in country now. We don't need all that bullshit here" he sighed.

"The captain's got the ass, and now I've got the ass too, but that ain't your fault. We have to move so many troops you can't believe it. There's a hundred thousand green recruits moving in every direction. Hell, we can't keep track of them all!"

A word had not yet escaped Casey's lips. He could feel heat penetrating his uniform and bugs crawling on his neck and inside his shirt sleeve. He tried to resist, but finally he slapped his neck, and then fetched a snout beetle from beneath his collar. "Sorry, Sergeant," he said.

"That's another thing, kid. There's Deet in your supplies. Use it. We wear long sleeve fatigues to keep the mosquitos off. You've got plenty of socks. Keep your feet dry. Jungle rot will kill you quicker than a company of them fuck'n gooks.

"I will." Casey said obediently.

"All the guys you came in with are truck drivers, clerks and cooks. You missed your convoy, but I've got good news. We've got a Huey pilot heading your way. He's a crazy sonofabitch they brought in to fuck with, to ground him, but for some odd reason they changed their minds. He's heading back out this afternoon. I'll have my clerk take you over there now."

He shouted, "Lopez. Get my jeep and get Private Rakestraw over to the airfield to meet a Huey we've got going back to the field."

The same clerk who had ushered Casey into the office entered the room. "Ah, is it Terry Smith?" he asked, a vague smile across his lips.

"Yep, the legend." Sergeant Beatty said.

As Corporal Lopez drove, he gave Casey the "skinny" on Terry Smith. "They brought him in to cite him with an Article15, for disobeying orders. He went into a firefight after he was ordered to stand down. He ignored the order and brought out six wounded. His co-pilot was hit so he left him with the wounded and went back in without a co-pilot to get sixteen more. When he came back in a Second Lieutenant tried to dress him down. Terry bloodied him up for his efforts. They grounded him and brought him in for discipline and to check out his rig to see if it was still flight worthy. Captain put him in for an Article 15."

"What's going on with him now?" Casey asked.

"General Westmoreland got wind of it and got the ass about it. He was pissed that Terry was confronted in the first place. He wasn't going to cite a fucking hero. The second Louie got disciplined and Terry got put in for a Distinguished Flying Cross."

"Sounds right," Casey said, grabbing the door handle as Lopez rounded a sharp corner.

"How'd you get so lucky to get a quick trip to the boonies?" Lopez asked, taking another sharp turn.

"I don't know, I'm just following orders," Casey said. At that moment they turned past the last hangar where F-15 fighter jets were lined up along the airstrip, and sixteen UH-1 (Huey) helicopters.

"That Huey with the bullet holes in it is your ride," Lopez said.

Heat rising from the asphalt was shimmering as a man advanced towards Casey in a mirage. A special effects movie scene - full cinematography. A gun belt with a forty-five caliber Smith and Wesson was slung over his shoulder, his chest bare, his skin a golden tan. A thick blond mop was protruding from beneath a straw cowboy hat. Terry Smith was the epitome of what

Hollywood actors could only hope to imitate.

"That's your man," Lopez said pointing at Terry, putting the Jeep into gear. "Thanks," Casey said, stepping aside.

Smith looked at Casey. He twisted a toothpick in his mouth, as he examined him. Casey said, "Sir, I'm supposed to catch a ride with you to my company outpost."

"I'm a Warrant Officer. Nobody calls me sir," he said. Casey didn't say anything. He waited for what came next. Terry turned towards the Huey. "Hop in," he said.

"Where do I sit?"

"Right there," Terry said, pointing to the co-pilot seat.

"Right there?" Casey asked, stunned. "Isn't there supposed to be a co-pilot, and some other guys?"

"Yep. Supposed to be a co-pilot, door gunner and a crew chief,"

"Are we picking them up"

"Nope, just you and me, Private." Terry said. A slight grin across his face.

The rotors began to accelerate, the blades created a dust cloud as the copter took flight. Casey's stomach was in his throat. As the copter tilted sideways, Casey grabbed at the air. Terry laughed. "Relax, man. I'm not gonna lose you."

There was radio chatter about a skirmish going on in the Central Highlands. A mountain range on the Vietnam/Cambodia border.

"Is that close?" Casey asked pointing to the radio.

"Everything is close. This country is only thirty miles wide in some places. I can get this flying grasshopper up to a hundred and thirty miles an hour when the wind is right. We can be in the Central Highlands in fifteen minutes," Terry said.

"But we won't, right? Casey said.

Before jumping into the co-pilot's seat, the war wasn't a reality to Casey. It was just training. A hurry up and wait kind of travel, and a lot of hassle from drill sergeants. Now suddenly it was front and center. Soldiers were killing each other in a place called the Central Highlands of Vietnam and it was only fifteen minutes away. The laugh, and the congenial smile Terry Smith was wearing when Casey was grabbing for the air was gone. Now there was a thousand-yard stare in his eyes.

"Maybe we'll take a look," Terry said

"Won't we need a gunner?" Casey stated. A nervous flick in his voice.

"I guess that's you," Terry said.

Casey stared at him in disbelief. He could feel the UH-1 changing directions. The rotors roaring, and the blades were beginning to make that signature rhythmic "whomping" sound as it accelerated.

"That gun is an M-60. That sonofabitch fires 500 rounds a minute," Terry said.

"I know what it is, but I've never fired one of 'um."

"You've fired an M-16, there's no difference. You point it and pull the trigger."

Casey's stomach was churning.

"Get back there and get that monkey harness on," Terry said.

"Don't you have to wait for orders" Casey shouted to be heard over the noise.

"I don't wait for orders. That's why they don't know

whether to ground me or give me a medal."

Viet Cong guerillas were camping in Cambodia and making raids in country. The First Calvary was patrolling the area along the border, finding small raiding parties but they usually retreated into the jungle without putting up a fight. Harassing outpost along the Ho Chi Ming Trail was their main objective, but recently they had been gathering steam. Support from regular North Vietnam Army troops coming down through Laos and Cambodia to give support to guerillas in the south had added strength to their capabilities. Terry Smith knew if that was the case the First Cav would be in deep shit. Radio traffic indicated they had been ambushed and were in retreat.

In a surreal moment Terry looked at Casey and said, "I'm Terry Smith. What's your name, kid?"

Casey's mind was racing. We're gonna be shot down. That's why he asked my name, he thought.

"Casey Rakestraw," he said. I'm nineteen years old, I work in a barn full of cow shit, but I don't want to die, he thought.

His eyes were focused on the mountains coming into view. They were covered by forest. At the base it was lush, flat and green. As they closed in the tall grass in the low ground looked like winter wheat swaying in the wind, wave upon wave. A little closer First Calvary troops were retreating with only their shoulders and combat helmets visible above the grass line. An overwhelming throng of guerillas and regular NVA were advancing on them. Casey couldn't hear the M-16's and the Chinese 53 carbines rattling, but he could see the smoke rising in the air from their gun barrels.

Terry shouted, "I'm flying across that field, I'll tilt

her over and you open fire!" He glanced at Casey who was strapped in, squatting on his haunches with the ammo canister between his legs, his face strained with fear visible in his eyes. "Just point and pull the trigger," Terry shouted.

Casey could feel the force when the copter turned and dropped nose down. He pointed the M-60 at the swarm of NVA soldiers advancing through the tall grass. When he opened fire, he could hear the whine of the gas and the hot lead from the M-60. The sound was like a pig squealing in a panic. In country the Americans called the M-60 the Hog. The Vietnamese called the Huey with an M-60, death from above. Both terms were appropriate.

NVA soldiers were dropping like flies or retreating. Casey's gut was churning, the muscles in his back were so tight he could feel the strain. He was shaking uncontrollably. Terry turned nose up and away from the action. "Are we done?" Casey shouted.

"No, we have to give that sixty a break. You'll melt the barrel. It takes two men to change the barrel in battle. We'll give it a break and then I'm going back in."

When they headed back in, Casey could see two dots on the horizon. When they got closer, he saw they were two Hueys at tree top level. Smoke rising from the M-60's at both doors. The NVA were retreating into the foliage in the tree line. One of the Hueys hovered and fired two missiles. A vapor trail formed behind them. The tree line went up in fire and smoke. Smoke covered the windscreen and boiled through the doorway. Terry turned away and gained altitude, swerving away to find relief from the black curtain forming in the air. Radio traffic from the other two Hueys indicated they would take it from there. They would pick up the wounded and get a body count. It was as routine as assigning household duties. You pick up the suits from the cleaners, I'll run the car through the car wash.

Terry didn't take Casey to his outpost. He flew into Bein Hoa where he and other pilots were living in villas off base. There were markets, clothing stores, restaurants and bars. American soldiers everywhere, mingling with Vietnamese. It wasn't the same war for Huey pilots as it was for the rest of the army. An apartment with a bed, couch and a tv room beat the hell out of hunkering down in a bunker. When a Pilot reported for duty many of them looked at it as just another day at the office. They started patrolling at dawn and finished at sunset. Airtime was restricted to 140 hours per month, so most of them were on duty one day, and off the next. Their time off was often spent in bars, and at their living quarters in their villas. Patrol was hours of boredom mixed with occasional moments of horror. Pilots were required to sign out and stay grounded for twenty-four hours.

The disadvantage was that a Huey pilot's life span during battle was nineteen minutes. When they lifted into the air, they knew it might be lights out before they were back on the ground.

Terry Smith wasn't just a Huey pilot with skin like iron. He was a maverick. He didn't always follow the rules. As far as he was concerned, he was always on duty. There were times when he took off alone without a co-pilot, crew chief or a door gunner. He cruised the jungle and the low ground looking for skirmishes where there might be wounded, and he followed patrols, staying alert for guys who stepped on booby traps. Maintaining scheduled hours meant nothing to him. His company commander realized Terry was uncontrollable, but he let him slide. He was the worst soldier, and the best, rolled into one gutsy sonofabitch. He knew Terry could not be changed. He admired Terry's courage and thought the United States military was lucky to have him. Terry had rescued more wounded soldiers than the rest of his company put together.

The company commander's clerk was waiting for Terry when his copter settled on the ground with Casey still sitting in the co-pilot seat. The dust and wind had him hunched forward, bending at the knees. He was holding his hat, his eyes closed, and a folder with papers tucked under his arm fluttering in the wind. When the rotors stopped, he approached Terry, an apprehensive expression on his face. "Terry, Captain Dee wants to know if you got Private Rakestraw to his outpost." Terry walked past him looking straight ahead.

"Nope," he said.

"What do you want me to tell the Captain, Terry?" he asked skittishly.

"Tell him I've still got him. I'll take him tomorrow, Henry - Tell him that." Terry said, spitting his toothpick onto the ground.

"Where are you going? Henry asked.

"Private Casey Rakestraw and I are going for a beer."

They caught a shuttle bus to a bar off base close to Terry's villa. The bar was dark inside. Budweiser, Stag, and Hamms neon lights hung against the walls behind the bar. Several other uniformed troops and guys dressed in civilian clothes were bellied up to the bar and sitting at tables. Other Huey pilots were there who had heard the radio traffic and asked about how things had turned out. They discussed it as if they were discussing a football game. Terry and another pilot played pool, they drank beer and plugged the juke box with quarters, playing songs by Johnny Cash, Loretta Lynn, and Waylon Jennings. Casey thought about what he had done. It seemed like a bad dream. Sitting there on a bar stool with his chin cupped in his hand trying to grasp the reality of it all.

Chapter Six

Special Agent Ford suspected there was a connection between Casey and Terry Smith. It was something that couldn't be found in military records, or anywhere else, but if he could prove what he suspected he could turn up the heat. Tyrese Green got out of his chair and walked to the window. Body language would indicate that he was getting disinterested. Casey had been questioned so many times if there was anyway of breaking him, it would have already happened. Casey could sense apathy in Greens demeanor, but Ford was still focused.

"Do you know how to fly a helicopter, Casey?" Agent Ford asked. Casey managed an impassive expression, but he knew where Ford was headed with the question.

"I'm not a licensed pilot, if that's what you're asking," Casey said.

"That wasn't the question. Do you know how to fly a helicopter?"

"How would I know how to do that?" Casey snorted.

The corners of Ford's mouth turned up slightly. He thought Casey's eyes shifted to the left, his lips formed a small circle at just the moment he closed his mouth. That was the first time he had done that during the entire questioning. Casey's shoulders moved slightly higher. He was getting ready to fold his arms across his chest before he caught himself. He's smart, Ford thought, but he's not superman.

Back in Vietnam friends were easy to find. Anybody who had your back was your best friend. Terry Smith was everybody's hero, but he was particular about who he hung out with. He liked Casey, and they became close friends. Casey was a "ground pounder," and it was unusual for Huey pilots to fraternize with anyone who wasn't a Huey operator, but that virgin flight Casey had made on his first day in country had bonded them together. Casey spent most of his time on patrol missions looking for Viet Cong guerillas, wading through rice paddies, and climbing mountainous jungles full of tropical plants, infested with insects and venomous snakes. There were guys who were killed by snipers and others had their legs blown off by booby traps. Casey was hardened to the fact it might be him at any moment. Occasionally mortar fire would send them diving into the weeds to lie in wait until the danger had passed. Casey was involved in only one blistering firefight, among many less dangerous encounters, and any of them might have spelled the end. He knew how to point his M-16 in the direction of enemy and fire. Their M-16's were rattling, jungle plants were being chopped off by hot led, and at times the bushes were thrashing about while being peppered with thousands of rounds of ammo. Casey never often saw Charley in the bush, but he fired in the right direction, and advanced when he was ordered to do it. The mud and heat and walking in wet boots was worse than dodging bullets and looking for booby traps.

Thoughts about the auction barn back in Illinois often crossed Casey's mind. He had never been as dirty shoveling pig shit, as when he was on patrol in Vietnam. At times he felt like one of those animals being herded into the center ring. Still, there were days when his platoon was back in camp for rest and recuperation. Terry Smith always found Casey at those times, and they had a few laughs. On one occasion after being in the jungle for days Casey's platoon was in base camp to recuperate. Casey didn't know what day of the week it was or even the month. Guerillas had been firing mortar rounds into base camp intermittently all morning. Nobody thought they were in danger of an attack, but they were cautious. Casey was in a bunker with three other guys. Two were passing a joint between them. The other was trying to write a letter. Casey closed his eyes and leaned his head against a sandbag. It was humid, damp, and as dark as a New York City subway but they were safe from mortar fire inside the bunker. Casey was about to doze when a mortar shell hit close enough to shake dust loose from the sandbags and rattle his teeth. Henry, a black guy that Casey liked a lot was one of the two guys hitting on a doobie. His eyes were bloodshot, and his eyelids were drooping. He had a great sense of humor, and he made Casey laugh even in the worst of times. Getting high when they had a break was standard operating procedure for Henry. When the mortar shell went off Henry scooted down farther in his stooped position. He giggled uncontrollably for a few moments and then took another hit on his marijuana roach. "I'm too short for Charley to get me now. Three weeks and I'm gone, man." He said, floating his hand in the air like a boat on a wave. The other guy was so stoned he snorted and laughed. Henry offered Casey a hit, but Casey shook his head, no. "Three weeks, man!" Henry said, sucking air and smoke along with his words deep into his lungs.

Casey smiled. "When Charley comes to get you, Henry, he won't care how short you are." Henry laughed again, coughing as though his lungs might come up. Casey leaned back again and closed his eyes. It wasn't long before he heard his name being called. "Casey, Rakestraw, there's a Huey Pilot out here looking for you." Casey opened his eyes and headed out into the bright sunlight. Terry Smith was sitting in the pilot seat of his UH-1 right there in the middle of the outpost. No co-pilot, no door gunner, no crew chief, just the man himself sitting there with the engine idling, shirtless, and smiling from beneath his cowboy hat. It was as likely as having a UFO landing, so several soldiers were rubber necking to see what was going on. They were used to seeing Huey's flying over on patrol, and transporting troops into and out of battle zones, but having a Huey just sitting there was a curious sight.

As he walked towards the copter one of the guys asked, "Who is that?"

"Terry Smith," Casey said.

"The legend in person, right here amongst us?" the guy asked.

"You got that right," Casey said.

Casey hopped into the co-pilot seat. "No crew?"

"Just you and me, buddy."

"What's going on?"

"I thought you might need to have a little fun. You're probably tired of burning villages and plundering the land," Terry said. Casey laughed.

When they lifted off the guys on the ground waved. They were all shirtless, wearing fatigue pants and camouflage army boots. Those long-sleeved fatigue uniforms Sergeant Beatty had told him to use to keep off the bugs had been discarded long ago. They were tanned by the sun, wearing the war, the crud and their worries on their faces. As they watch the UH-1 rising they resembled little kids watching a Ferris wheel leaving with their friends aboard while they waited in line on the ground. They all needed some fun, and Terry Smith was about to deliver it.

Terry flew out a few miles and then hovered. "Casey, I've got a thick blue cord lying back by the gunner's door. I need for you to get in the monkey harness and attach it to the cord.

"Why? Are you gonna lower me to the ground?" Casey asked, a puzzled expression on his face.

"It's a bungy cord. You're gonna jump out. It's like a giant rubber band."

" Why would I wanna do that!"

Terry laughed. "You've never had so much fun, Casey. You're out there in the wind bouncing like you're on an invisible trampoline!"

"I'm not doing it."

"Come on, man, you'll always wonder what you missed if you don't give it a try. I've done it. It's better than parachuting."

'I've never done that either. I'm not a crazy sonofabitch like you, Terry. You're not afraid of anything," irritation rising in his voice.

Terry's expression changed, that one-thousand-yard stare in his eyes. His brow furrowed. "I'm afraid of everything, Casey. Every time I get in this flying grasshopper it scares me. Every time I fly into a firefight, I think it might be my last flight. I'm scared all the time, Casey."

Casey peered at his friend. He couldn't conceive

such a thought. He waited for Terry to continue, but he was silent. Casey exhaled, "Okay, I'll do it, God damnit! "

I knew you would," Terry said grinning.

"Where?"

"I've got the perfect place."

Ten minutes later they were flying over Casey's base camp. The bungy cord was lying in a neat pile with the metal hook and rod attached to the rescue wench. Casey was crouched in the open doorway. He was shaking like a terrified dog. When he saw his fellow soldiers on the ground, he took a deep breath and jumped. Wind passing by his ears was like thunder. His rib and back muscles were so tight they were aching. When he released the air from his lungs, he could hear himself yelling but he didn't recognize his own voice. As he approached the end of the cord he thought, God don't let me hit the ground!

When he felt the tug, and then a momentary hesitation, he released a cackle like a carnival clown at the dunk tank. High and dry! He could feel himself turning sideways, weightless in the wind, lifting higher, and higher. In another moment he could sense his speed slowing down, and then another pause before heading downward. He was bouncing, just like Terry said, he was on a giant rubber band! The guys on the ground were laughing and shouting as if they were watching the Flying Wallendas!

He was up and down like a yoyo for what seemed like forever, but it was only minutes. When he was nearly still, swaying slightly, Terry winched him back up into the copter. They were both laughing like little kids in a giggling fit. It was the most exhilarating experience in Casey's life. That memory would stay with him forever. When Terry set down on the ground at Casey's outpost, troops surrounded the copter, cheering Casey as they would have a conquering hero.

Chapter Seven

Terry Smith taught Casey how to fly a UH-1 helicopter. It may have been unprecedented in the history of the Vietnam war, and unauthorized, but he did it. That was the point Agent Ford wanted to establish. Having the ability to fly a helicopter was crucial to the ISG Museum heist. It was also something the general public didn't know. Having a pilot's license didn't matter to Ford. Just pinning Casey down to being able to operate a helicopter was crucial.

The first time Casey tried to get off the ground he lightly pulled up the collective and the Huey shot to the right and went into a spin. Terry chuckled as the big bird spun around, blowing dirt and leaves like a giant lawn mower on a dust trail. Terry let it ride until Casey shouted, "Fuck this!" Terry hit the rudder pedals to bring it under control. "I'm getting out!" Casey said. "You gotta give it a chance, Casey. Nobody gets it the first try."

Casey sat staring straight ahead, his lips tight across his teeth. Terry tapped him across his shoulder with the back of his hand. A smile beaming like a mother encouraging her toddler to be brave. Casey snickered, rubbed his hands together and grabbed the cyclic control. That was the official name, but it was just the stick to him. He watched the control panel until the engine was registering 1500 rpms. He raised the collective putting a little forward pressure on the stick he started moving forward. The Huey was again moving to the right, Casey swallowed hard, waiting for it to go into another violent spin. "Put a little pressure on the left rudder pedal," Terry said. Casey gingerly pushed down on the pedal, and it corrected. He laughed a quiet little laugh way down in his throat. When they were airborne, Casey was surprised how easy it was to glide through the air. Casey was leaning forward with his back straight, looking as though watching traffic, ready to apply the brakes. Slight pressure to the right, you veered to the right. If you raised the collective, you got a gentle lift and an increase in speed. Casey chuckled like a kid.

"Just like flying a plane, right, Casey?"

"I've never flown a plane, Terry, but I'm starting to like this!"

They were in the air for an hour. Terry pointed out locations where Charley might be hiding, and trails used by platoons on patrol. Casey veered left and right, picked up speed and gained altitude. He was comfortable in the pilot's seat.

That was the first time Casey piloted a Huey, but it wasn't the last. Terry continued to teach Casey until he was proficient enough to fly alone. Every time they went up it was reason to Court Marshall them both and to ground Terry for good, but it never happened. Everybody in Casey's platoon knew about it, but it was as if Terry Smith was immune – invulnerable.

Casey continued to fight the war. He went on patrol, dove into ditches to avoid being killed in surprise attacks and stayed alert for booby traps. He got used to being filthy in his fatigues, his feet were wet most of the time, and he accepted being uncomfortable. He burned villages and fired his M-16 in the right direction. Casey never felt justified in his actions, but it was a war, and he was a soldier.

Terry Smith was shot down on February 7th, 1968, in the battle of Lo Gaing. His name is engraved on the Vietnam Memorial wall in Washington DC.

The last time Casey saw Terry he was sitting in the pilot seat alone. He was looking at Casey through the side window with a warm expression on his face. The corners of his lips turned up slightly, and a knowing countenance in his eyes. As Terry lifted off the ground, Casey waved goodbye. Casey never had a friend in his life that he valued as much as Terry Smith.

Casey did his time, honorably, but it had taken a toll on his view of the US government, and especially the President. Body counts were more important than anything else. After being in Vietnam for a year Casey had the impression there would never be an end to it. Viet Cong guerillas were never going to give up, the insurgency in the south was growing, and the American public weren't on the side of the soldiers who were fighting and dying there.

While waiting to be shipped out from Bien Hoa air base Casey and some other guys were in a bar celebrating ending their tour in Vietnam. The war was still raging, but they were through with it. They were all going home. Most of them were drunk. Tables full of American soldiers laughing and hitting on Vietnamese prostitutes who would just take their money and then disappear. It was a party like atmosphere, but strangely there was a sense of separation. The bar was filled with smoke and dreary even in the glow of the neon lights. Casey wasn't celebrating. He was thinking about all the guys who had been killed. And then through the purple haze, he saw a slender young man approaching his table. It was Shaky Jake Brenner!

Casey smiled. He wondered if Jake had spent his time in Vietnam huddling in a bunker avoiding the war, but here he was, looking just like he did back in the states. "What the hell!" he said, standing and offering his hand. Jake laughed out loud. "We're still alive!"

Casey didn't have an attachment to Jake, he barely knew him, but strangely it was like finding an old friend. "Sit down," he said, sliding an extra beer he had across the table. Jake took a chair, and then they both laughed again. They talked about basic training as if it had been the most eventful thing they had done during their tour. Casey didn't want to think about the guys with their legs blown off, or soldiers dying, asking for promises to tell their parents that they loved them. He didn't want to relive wading through rice paddies or huddling in ditches trying to find where the sniper fire was coming from. Casey was glad he was going home, but he knew the war was still going on and there were guys just like him, out there fighting for something few people appreciated.

Finally, Jake asked Casey where he had been.

"All over," Casey said, spoken in a way to indicate there was nothing more to say about it.

"How about you?" he asked, throwing the conversation back to Jake.

"Here, I've been right here in Bien Hoa. I'm in supply. I've been here on base most of the time."

Makes sense, Casey thought.

"What are you gonna do when you get back home?" Jake asked.

"Go back to shoveling shit, I guess," Casey said, chuckling slightly. "What about you"

"I'll go back to my old job, maybe. I was a security guard in Boston. I went back home to Illinois when I got my draft notice."

Casey couldn't believe what he heard. He couldn't imagine Jake in an occupation where he would have to safeguard anything. What kind of business would hire Jake for protection, he thought. A tinge of guilt radiated across his face. Jake lacked courage, but he wasn't dumb. He read the expression on Casey's face. "It wasn't a dangerous job," he said.

"I didn't know I was that easy to read. I'm sorry, Jake." Casey said.

"I'm a big chicken, everybody knows that." He giggled.

"I knew a security guard who worked in a factory back home. He did things like check fire extinguishers and do safety checks. I guess not all security jobs are dangerous." Casey said.

"I never really thought about anything happening to me. I was barely twenty-one, and it was in a privately owned museum on a college campus. There was a bunch of lightweights like me in the neighborhood. Seniors and intellectuals were the only people who came in. Occasionally a college class came through but there was never any trouble. At night we locked up and nobody could come in." Jake said.

"Just old junk and statues and stuff like that?"

"No, man, they had Picasso. Rembrandt, and a bunch of famous artists from all over. There were Civil war relics, and stuff from the Conquistadores in South America. There was a helmet worth three hundred thousand dollars. The Picassos and Rembrandts were worth several hundred million." Jake said.

Casey was just a country boy, but he was savvy enough to know that valuables like that shouldn't be left for Shaky Jake Brenner to secure. He was fascinated by everything Jake said, and he would remember it. Casey was twenty-one, and Jake was twenty-three. That conversation would someday shape Casey's future.

Chapter Eight

Casey was right about the weather. The trees along the lake were nearly shrouded by a white curtain of snow. A sudden gust blew open the office door spreading dry leaves across the floor. Agent Green leapt from his chair to grab the door and slam it shut. He rubbed one arm and then the other, trying to rub off the chill, exhaling heavily.

"A wind breaker here in Wisconsin won't keep off the cold," Casey said.

Agent Ford got up and paced around the office. Pictures of boats, docks, and men proudly holding fish they had caught lined the walls. Paint was peeling in several places. The windows were old, cracked and dirty.

"Casey, this is off the subject, but how did you end up here?" Ford asked, frowning.

"Just lucky, I guess," Casey said.

Ford cocked his head sideways, his brow furrowing. "You're a lawyer. You graduated Suma cum Laude at the University of Illinois law school. I'd think you'd be in a fancy downtown Chicago office building instead of here in a little boat shop, freezing, with nothing to keep you warm besides a little kerosene heater," he said.

"I thought you were here to find out how I robbed the Ida Swigert Graham Museum, Agent Ford? Not to disparage the surroundings."

"Why don't you tell me then? Greene and I can get

out of the cold and start our tv and radio tour for solving the most infamous crime in our history," Ford said.

"I've denied having anything to do with that heist in a thousand ways. If you're depending on me to tell you how it happened, you'll have a long wait." Casey said. He paused for a long moment. "I've been asked by CNN and Fox News both to do an interview about how you guys keep harassing me, but I turned them down. So, maybe we can be friends," he said sarcastically.

It had been a long road to this little office on the lake, bumpy at times, and risky, but Casey had lived life on his own terms. When he deplaned in Oakland, California on his flight from Bien Hoa, he and eighty fellow soldiers were walking across the tarmac when they were met by college students protesting the war. Behind the chain link fence signs were being waved in the air. Baby Killer, in black letters with red paint drops below the declaration, implying blood was on their hands. Kids were spitting in his direction and shouting murderer!

Before they reached the gate, the air was rife with round balls being flung from beyond the fence. Casey was hit in the chest and shoulder. He covered his head with folded arms until the barrage ended. He picked up one of the balls. "This is horse shit!" he growled. A guy next to him said, "You got that right."

"No, this is really horse shit! These are turds!" Casey said.

"Well, bullshit!" the guy uttered in disgust.

Casey felt dejected. While he waited for the military bus to transport them to the Oakland Army Terminal, he mulled over everything that had transpired since the last time his feet were on American soil. Oakland,

California sure wasn't Delavan, Illinois, but people were basically the same wherever you were. The world was a big place. He thought he had seen the worst of it already, but nothing hurt like being hit with horse turds thrown by his fellow Americans.

In those quiet moments in the terminal his thoughts meandered through his past. Moving around from one little town to the other was like being on a rudderless ship drifting on an open sea. Back then he never gave his future a thought. He had read everything he could get his hands on, but it wasn't to prepare him for life. It was just to feed his curiosity. Now as he sat there with horse shit stains on his uniform, thinking about the young people spitting at him, he thought, I could actually be better than those idiots, and better than I am!

The Federal GI Bill was available to all veterans, and the State of Illinois had a free educational program for GI's who entered the military as a resident and returned to Illinois after discharge. Maybe he could do that. He had survived Vietnam; college should be a cake walk.

It took Casey eight years to get his bachelor's degree and a degree in law from the University of Illinois. The extra year was because he had to attend a community college in Springfield, taking classes in subjects required by the university in order to be eligible. He started as a freshman at the U of I in 1970 and graduated in 1978. By that time lawyers were a dime a dozen. You couldn't sling a cat without hitting a lawyer in Springfield, Illinois. He eked out a mere living, and it was easy to see he was never going to be one of those high-profile attorneys who were rolling in dough. It made it easy to get dates, because women were impressed with the profession, and at parties, he was often the center of attention. That was never enough for Casey, but that wasn't the reason he ended up in his little frigid boat shop in Wisconsin.

All of that was streaming through Casey's memory as Agent Ford was wandering around the office gawking at the black and white pictures on the walls. Agent Green was at the window, his gaze fixed watching little vortex of snow traveling across the roadway in front of their car. He chewed on his lower lip, obviously concerned about being stranded in the backwoods of Wisconsin.

Agent Ford walked near Casey. He pushed both hands into his front pockets and looked down at him. Casey was in his chair. He looked up at Ford. "What the hell are you looking at," he thought. Ford smiled. "Do you still practice law? He asked.

"Not really, but when I hear about some poor guy who's getting railroaded, I work pro bono. I've kept a few innocent guys from going to jail"

"Do you wear your flannel shirt, and your life is good cap to court?"

"I've got an Armani suit and a pair of Louis Vuitton shoes for special occasions," Casey said.

"Really?"

"No, not really! I've never even seen a pair of Louis Vuitton shoes. Beside that you probably know every case I ever defended. You've been looking at me for twenty-five years. Didn't you read my file? Don't they review all that stuff and make notes before they send a new team out here to fuck with me?

"We know about the Jason Keys case. Why don't you tell us about that?" Agent Green said, turning away from the window.

"I don't know what you're talking about. Why don't you get a court transcript? Since you're the FBI you can probably get a free copy," Casey said.

"It wasn't exactly a trial, was it?" Ford said, turning to study Casey's expression. Casey looked back. His eyes were saying, "I know where you're going with this, but it ain't gonna fly.

"I sort of remember a Civil Service Commission hearing. I think the guy's name was Keys. He was a cop they were fuck'n with. I tried to save his job, but you can't fight City Hall.

Jason Keys was a Vietnam veteran. He volunteered in 1971 with the intention of making a career of the military. He was twenty years old when he signed his enlistment papers. After spending a year in Vietnam, seeing respect for war veterans deteriorate, and being exposed to incompetent leadership, his desire to serve had vanished. When he returned to the states, he was assigned to a Military Police unit working downtown St. Louis, Missouri, in the 5th Army headquarters. There wasn't much law enforcement involved in his duties. Fetching high ranking officers from Lambert Field and participating in twenty-one-gun salutes at military funerals at Jefferson Barracks kept him busy. Nothing about it resembled police work but it motivated him to seek law enforcement as a profession.

After being discharged in 1974 Jason enrolled in community college in Springfield, Illinois in order to qualify to take the test for patrolman. He graduated with an associate degree in 1976. Five months later he was in the police academy. He served seven years before his world was turned upside down.

On May 20th, 1983, at 3 am, the mythical black cat of bad luck crossed the roadway to his future. His partner had called in sick, so he was working alone. Springfield is as quiet as a graveyard at 3 in the morning. Not even Abraham Lincoln's ghost stirs in the Old State Capitol after the sidewalks have been rolled up. The bars close at two, and the drunken brawls in the projects usually run out of steam by that time. Jason was parked at North Grand Avenue and Ninth Street in the Illinois Environmental Protection Agency parking lot. Hidden between two research trucks, he was nearly invisible. An Illinois Revised Statutes volume was in his lap and a binder of Illinois Annotated Case Law in the passenger seat. Taking advantage of the quiet he was studying for the upcoming sergeant's exam.

It had rained earlier. The streets were damp, and a vanilla glow hung in the low clouds over the city. The dome on the state capitol was lit up and glistening against the blackened sky. Jason rubbed his eyes. They were burning from reading in the dim light in the squad car. It was peaceful. He was thinking about grabbing coffee at McDonalds to fight off the drowsiness. It was just another boring night on the graveyard shift. The problem was in the old cliché, hours of boredom and moments of terror.

Jason was just exiting his hiding place between the EPA trucks when he could hear the whine of an engine accelerating. There were three cars sitting at the traffic light on Ninth, and a Chicago Tribune box truck on North Grand. Jason could still hear the engine accelerating. He could see a black BMW eastbound on North Grand. If it had wings it would have been airborne. When the light changed the three cars waiting began to move forward. A blast from the BMW's horn was like a freight train approaching a railroad crossing. Jason was expecting screeching tires, metal scraping and shattering glass. A disaster seemed inescapable. The BMW skidded sideways and jumped the curb. The other cars had stopped, the drivers must have been screaming inside their heads because they didn't have a millisecond to react. The BMW careened back onto the street, fishtailing from one side of the road to the other miraculously missing the cars and traffic controls. Blue smoke was rising from the tires as the rubber screeched across the concrete.

Jason activated his emergency lights and siren, at the same time transmitting the situation to dispatch. He didn't ask for backup; it was automatic. The BMW careened into the Springfield Sliders parking lot on two wheels, coming to a stop between the concrete supports.

Jason was out of his car, shoving his night stick into the ring on his belt. With one hand on his nine-millimeter the other arm outstretched, his index finger pointing at the driver. "Stay in your car, shut off the engine and hand me the keys!" He shouted. Inside the car sitting behind the steering wheel a young man was laughing like a hyena. "Go fuck yourself," he said. His eyes were mere slits, and saliva dripped from his mouth.

"Stay in your car, shut off the engine and hand me the keys," Jason said sternly. " I'm not giving them to you," the guy responded.

"Give me the keys! You're under arrest."

"Move your little toy squad car and I'll be on my

way," the guy sneered.

"Turn off the engine and give me your keys!" Jason demanded; irritation audible in his voice.

"Do you know who I am!" the guy said, with an air of superiority as evident as his drunkenness.

Jason bit his lower lip. It wouldn't make a difference in how he was going to handle the situation, but he knew there were always problems with, do you know who I am, declarations.

"I had dinner with the governor this evening. I just donated a stove pipe hat to the Abraham Lincoln Museum worth ten million dollars. Lincoln wore it to Ford's Theatre the night he was assassinated. You'll be in deep shit when the governor hears about this," the guy slurred.

"Shut off the engine and give me the keys," Jason said again.

At that point, the guy cracked open the door and shoved it open with as much strength as he could muster. The door swung open striking Jason, knocking him backwards. Even in his drunken condition the guy was able to exit the car, but his knees gave out on the way. He grabbed at Jason for support. He was like a piece of linguini swaying from side to side. His left hand latched onto Jason's shoulder and his right hand went for the nightstick dangling on Jason's belt. Instinctively Jason grabbed the baton and loosened it from the guy's hand. At some point between the time he grabbed for the nightstick and tumbling to the asphalt his head came into contact with the sideview mirror. Blood was streaming down his left cheek and running into his sideburn.

At that very moment backup arrived. Jason was

standing over the man who was lying on his back in a daze with blood oozing from his head. Jason had his nightstick in his hand. When the backup squad car lights hit upon Jason, he looked like a Gestapo storm trooper giving a helpless Jew a good whacking.

The guy was taken to the police station for booking on Reckless Driving and Driving Under the Influence. Before he could be printed and photographed, the mayor and chief of police were there. Instead of filing his reports Jason was contacted by the shift sergeant and ordered to go to the Chief's office. The, do you know who I am, statement had manifested into a full-blown catastrophe.

The guy's name was Dean Allen Marlo, the son of an independent art collector and owner of the ISG Museum. He had traveled from Boston to donate a stove pipe hat that belonged to Abraham Lincoln. As a collector's item it was valued at several million dollars – a small sum for the ISG Museum. The museum was worth billions. Picasso, Rembrandt, Monet, and a plethora of other famous dead artist were hanging on the walls. Artifacts from ancient Rome, and the Napoleonic wars were all exhibits contained within the ISG Museum walls. Marlo did in fact have dinner with the governor less than eight hours before he rampaged through the intersection where Jason found him in a drunken stupor behind the wheel of a rented BMW. To say that Jason had the misfortune of being at North Grand and Ninth Street when Dean Allen Marlo soared past the red light was an understatement.

Jason was suspended pending a civil service hearing. He was charged with Conduct Unbecoming a Police Officer, and Unnecessary Use of Force.

Three days after the incident, Casey Rakestraw was meeting Billy Wiley in the Sunrise Café just down the street from the Sangamon County Courthouse. Billy had been evicted from a rundown house on south Tenth Street by the Sheriff's Department. In the process Billy became rowdy and spit on a deputy while he was reading Billy the eviction order. The cops roughed him up and placed him under arrest for Disorderly Conduct. Casey was on the list to represent indigent defendants and received his fee from the county. He caught Billy Wiley's case as a client in the rotation.

Casey had been working for a downtown law firm for five years, but the drivel in a law firm was nothing more than a bunch of hogwash. He wasn't suited for small claims cases, and petty lawsuits against insurance companies offended his sense of decency. He felt like a whore every time he billed a client. The firm looked over his shoulder making sure he billed every phone call and rounded one minute to a quarter of an hour. A license to steal was not a misappropriated terminology. Young lawyers in their three-piece suits having three fingers of scotch at three pm after swindling farm family heirs out of their land, was parr for the course. Casey wasn't cut out for that. Now his office was in his car; his files were manila envelopes stacked in the back seat. His clients were indigents, traffic offenders, and drunks. Casey had been sought after by several firms in the city, but he knew they were all the same, and his answer was always no.

When Billy came into the café, Casey was sitting at a table having coffee, reviewing Billy's file. Billy spoke to every person within hearing distance. He was about as intimidating as one of the seven dwarfs. His cheeks were rosy, his eyebrows were like two fuller brushes, and a little round nose like a ping pong ball. "Hi, Joey, hi, Milly! How's it going Jake? I heard you won five hundred on a scratch off. I'll bet that feels good!" His voice a high-pitched squeal, but somehow it wasn't annoying. The irritating sound of it was mitigated by his cheerful tone and the good nature bubbling from it.

There were two city cops sitting at the counter having coffee. Billy stopped and gawked at them with raised eyebrows. They both eyed him with passive smiles as they would have a harmless puppy waiting for attention. "Hey, Billy," they said in unison.

"Hey, officers," Billy said. He looked at them until they turned back toward the counter. When he saw Casey, he pulled at his belt loops and aligned his gig line higher on his stomach. "Hi, Mr. Rakestraw, my lawyer friend," he said in a voice loud enough for people nearby to hear. A more innocent looking soul had never found his way into the criminal court system. Any of the Muppets on CBS could have used him as a stand in.

As he sat down, he said, "Cops are good people."

Casey smiled. "I guess if they're throwing you out on the street it can get under your skin a little," he said.

"Yeah, but I was wrong," Billy said.

After a short conversation they agreed to go before the judge, plead guilty, and ask for Court Supervision. Casey was certain that once the judge looked at Billy, it was a done deal. During their conversation he was eavesdropping on the two cops. What they were saying was interesting to Casey. It was about Jason Keys' problems with the rich guy who was trying to destroy his life. Jason had done nothing more than his job, but the department had thrown him under the bus.

As Casey was leaving the café, he stopped at the counter and handed one of the cops his card. "Tell your buddy, I'll represent him at his hearing, pro bono."

That moment would bring Casey, Jason and Billy back together in the future.

Chapter Nine

Agent Green was at the window again. He wiped the steam off the glass with his hand. "Lee we may have to cut this short. The snow is really piling up out there. I don't want to be stranded out here," he said. Agent Ford ignored him.

"The case with Jason Keys didn't go well," Ford said rhetorically.

"He lost his job. Two kids, a mortgage, you know, the whole works. I wanted to save his job, but I guess you already know how it went." Casey said, tightening his lower lip.

"You can't fight city hall," Ford said.

"The sonofabitch didn't even show up for the hearing. He did send me a note threatening to have me disbarred," Casey said.

Lee Ford put both hands in his pockets again. "You do know why I mention Jason Keys, don't you?"

"I guess it's because the scum bag he arrested owns the ISG Museum, and he's the no-good sonofabitch who's responsible for Jason Keys demise. I did that heist to get even, right? That's a stretch, Lee." Casey stood up and with both hands he gestured a banner over his head. "Casey Rakestraw robs ISG Museum in an act of revenge for his client!" He laughed at his own antics before sitting back down.

"It fits the scenario," Ford said. Green was distracted from watching the snow just long enough to say, "People have screwed up their lives for less."

"My life is not screwed up, Tyrese," Casey said.

Green raised his eyebrows and glanced around the room in an exaggerated manner, suggesting that maybe it was. Casey watched his eyes. He got it. It was shabby, but it was by design. Casey had a plan, but even without that, this was better than what was expected of him as an attorney. He was a lawyer in good standing. He could change everything in the blink of an eye, He could slither back into the swamp with the other lawyers who were charging clients fifteen minutes for every minute on the quarter hour. Old dying women in nursing homes still need executors of their estates. He could legally find ways to swindle their heirs out of every dime they had coming to them. He could defend murderers who were guilty, suborn perjury and find ways to make every innocent witness look like serial liars in court. He could do all of that, but he preferred his drab little office in the sticks.

"We've been through a litany of names, Casey. What do you think so far"? Ford said.

"I don't know about all that. I'll bet I could find people who you knew throughout your life that could be mixed into a brew of bizarre events that were a little cockeyed. It might make your association with them look suspicious. They say we're all only seven people removed from Kevin Bacon," Casey said with a slight smile.

"Yeah, sure enough, but put all these things together and they start to paint a picture, Casey. We think there was a helicopter involved in the heist. Terry Smith was your best friend in Nam. He taught you how to fly a Huey,"

"You don't know that. That would be against every

rule in the book. We both would have been court-martialed if anything like that happened. Besides that, you guys have been here how many times? That's the first time anyone mentioned a helicopter, "Casey said.

"We talked to a guy by the name of Henry Burchett who says he saw you flying a copter first-hand," Green said. Ford gave him a perturbed glance. Green rolled his eyes.

"Yeah, I remember Henry. He was the one flying most of the time and it wasn't a helicopter," Casey chuckled.

"You were buds with Jake Brenner, and he just happened to have been a guard at the ISG Museum before he was drafted. And then there was the Jason Keys incident. Do you see the picture, Casey?"

"Is that all you've got, Agent Ford?" Casey shrugged and raised his eyebrows.

"Why are you so nonchalant about all this, Casey? Most people would worry a little bit knowing the circumstantial evidence is starting to look like a wildfire. Why don't you mention making a deal, just write it all down and we'll make it easier on you," Ford said.

"Not today, Agent Ford. Not today."

"That's not all I've got, Casey. How about Savanah Anderson?

"My God, how would you know about Savanah Anderson? I knew the girl for two weeks. She must be 65 years old by now!" Casey thought

"You knew her pretty well, didn't you, Casey?"

"I can't say I knew anyone by that name," Casey said.

Agent Ford laughed at Casey's answer.

Lying was distasteful to Casey, but so was robbery, and by the evidence he was guilty of both. The year was 1995. ISG Heist was unsolved, and still number one on the FBI's most wanted list. Savanah Anderson was a small but important part of it.

Casey met Savanah Anderson in Maple Creek, a quiet little town in Oklahoma. He was there closing a purchase for a client on a future golf course. Casey was a little out of his element. He was still working out of his car, but everybody knew he was a smart guy, and more than that, he was honest. He preferred defending indigents, and people down on their luck, but paying the bills required sometimes rubbing elbows with the upper crust. When all the contracts were signed, he stopped in the Midland Café for lunch. Savanah was sitting in a booth. Casey sat at the counter. He glanced at her. She was thin, brown hair, beautiful smooth skin, and the deepest brown eyes he had ever seen. She watched Casey with interest – studying him. She liked his looks. The suit he was wearing was something you would find on the rack at Sears, but it fit like it was tailor-made just for him. The way he walked and held himself breathed confidence. He was tall, but not too tall. His eyebrows were thick and dark, and his shoulders were broad. Casey was exactly what she was looking for. Savanah didn't know how to flirt. Going straight forward was the only thing she knew how to do. She took a pen from her purse and wrote a note on a paper napkin. I'll meet you outside, it said. As she walked by the counter, she placed it face down in front of him. Casey watched her walk to the door. She was wearing a burnt umber cotton sleeveless dress. It was something you would never see in Chicago, or even

Springfield, Illinois. She was gliding with her arms stiff at her sides. Her hips were clearly moving with each step, enunciated by the soft cotton material of her dress. Casey's heart was in his throat.

When he stepped out of the restaurant, Savanah was standing, resting her back against a 1985 Silverado pickup truck. Casey walked up and stopped. "What's this all about?" He asked.

"I don't know any other way of doing this. I want you to come to my farm. I just want to have an afternoon with you. I like the way you look. It's that simple," Savanah said.

"I don't know. I've never done anything like that. I've disappointed women. Women that I actually know, so I'm not sure. I wouldn't want you to think I'm some stud looking for a one-night stand," Casey said laughingly. He couldn't believe someone as beautiful as Savanah would put forth such a proposal.

"I live at 1833 County Road Z," she said, opening the door to the Silverado. When she drove away, Casey had butterflies in his stomach. Was this real, or just a scheme to embarrass him? It took an hour before Casey decided he would drive by the address Savanah had given him. Casey wasn't one of those guys who thought of himself as God's gift to women. He was a confident guy. He was an attorney, he had walked through gunfire and mine fields in Vietnam, he knew how to fly a helicopter, he wasn't afraid of any man, but women made him a little nervous.

It was a long gravel lane with green pastures on each side of the road. There were hills and trees in the distance. It was a beautiful place. There was a two-story farmhouse with a picket fence around it, a smoke house and a barn. It was the typical rural family dwelling. When Casey stopped in the lane Infront of the picket fence, Savanah was standing on the porch. Casey got out of the car and started towards the house. He noticed the mailbox, marked, Kenneth and Savanah Anderson. As he walked onto the porch he asked, "Are you Savanah?"

"Let's not do names," Savanah said.

"Okay," Casey said, looking at Savanah with a subtle smile. "I'm not good at these things," he added.

"I'm not good at them either, I've never done anything like this, and I don't really know what I'm doing now," she said. Her expression was so earnest that Casey was left speechless. There was something about her that he couldn't explain, but he couldn't resist.

"You can call me Savanah because you read my mailbox. I'll call you Simon," she said.

"Okay," Casey said.

"We'll have coffee. Come inside."

Casey sat at the kitchen table while Savanah talked about the farm. She had free-range chickens, two goats that ate nothing but brush, a cow that she had to milk every day regardless of her ability to use all the milk, and a garden with pole beans, sweet corn, potatoes, tomatoes, and squash. She had a well with a pump and a field full of sunflowers. She gave the excess milk to the rural mail carrier. Sometimes she would laugh. It came from down in her throat, so mellow, and real, that Casey could feel it somewhere inside his gut.

"I wear gloves to keep my hands from getting calloused," she said.

"Who's Kenneth Anderson? Casey asked,

interrupting.

"My husband,"

"Where is he?"

"He's on a pheasant hunting trip with his brother. They're going to be in Colorado for two weeks. When he gets back the sheriff will be serving him with divorce papers," Savanah said.

"Does he know?"

"Not yet, but I'm sure he'll be relieved. He has a girlfriend in town. I think she's pregnant," Savanah said.

"I'm sorry," Casey said.

"I'm not. She's a nice girl. I feel sorry for her though. He thinks he's in love with her. It won't last. He doesn't know how to love anyone."

They sat in silence for a long time. Casey was watching Savanah without being able to turn away. She was beautiful, but it was the other thing that fascinated him. It was that thing he couldn't put his finger on that was pulling him in.

"Simon, will you sleep with me tonight?"

Casey didn't answer immediately. Savanah looked at him like no one had ever looked at him before. She was studying his expression and at the same time conveying a look of wonder. It was like she was seeing everything about him in that single gaze.

"I don't mean sexually. I just want you to sleep in my bed with me," she said.

"Yes, I will," he said.

Casey slept with Savanah, and it turned out to be sexual. It was the most rewarding experience of his life. It was the same every night and sometimes during the day for thirteen days. When he looked at her, he wanted to absorb her – to consume her. He had never been in love before, and it had surprised him.

He learned to milk a cow, hoe the garden, and feed chickens. He wanted every day to last forever. Maybe this was what he wanted when he was a young man moving around from one little town to another, looking for fulfillment. He certainly wasn't happy as a lawyer. You could get dirty here, but you were still clean on the inside. Still, he knew it would end because she had told him so. She was direct about everything, and she never lied.

Sunlight was casting an orange glow over the horizon. Chickens were pecking in the dirt as Savanah pitched ground corn across the yard. Casey walked out of the house with the screen door slamming behind him. It was loud enough for her to hear him, but she didn't turn to look. He had on the same suit he was wearing when he arrived. He walked up beside her and reached into the coffee can for a handful of corn and pitched it into the dirt. The chickens furiously pecked and scratched at the ground.

"I could stay here, Savanah," he said.

Savanah didn't answer. She threw more corn from the coffee can. "The crows are devastating my tomatoes," she said quietly.

"I could open up a little office in Maple Creek. I'm sure people around here need wills and land titles. Maybe even a county contract for legal services," Casey said.

"Simon, I'm never going to be in love again. It's too painful. If you stay, it's inevitable. I can't do it," Savanah said. Casey was certain that she already loved him, and he was in love with her, but he knew he wasn't going to change her mind.

"Those crows are annoying too. In the morning they could wake the dead with their constant squawking." she said.

Casey walked to his car and popped the trunk. He retrieved a metal helmet with a steel feather rising from the back side of the base. When he came back, he walked into the garden and gathered straw and sticks and placed them on the ground near a fence post. He went into the house and brought back a hammer and nail. He found a stick long enough to reach across the post an equal length on both sides and nailed it to the post. There was a hollow gourd on the ground. It was just the right size for a head, He shoved the straw and sticks inside the helmet and then the hollow gourd. He took off his jacket and filled it with straw and hung it on the stick across the fence post. When it was done it was an excellent looking scarecrow.

He walked back to Savanah with a longing in his eyes. There was a dulcet smile on her lips, but it was sad too. There was an expression of acceptance and of loss in that expression - a hollow victory.

"I guess I better go," Casey said, watching her face, waiting for a signal that she wanted him to stay.

"I guess you should," she said.

As Casey drove away, he saw Savanah in the rearview mirror trimming the scarecrow.

Chapter Ten

Agent Ford rubbed his hands together. The kerosene heater was losing the battle with the cold air in the cabin. Casey was leaning back in his chair, still relaxed and confident.

"We talked to Savanah Anderson not long ago, Casey," Ford said. "It was a long time coming but we finally got a lead on her. It was in a file right there in front of us for years. On May 2. 1999 there were 74 tornados across Oklahoma and Kansas. It tore the hell out of everything. One of the places that got hit was Maple Creek, Oklahoma. They had video of everything for days on the Weather Channel. It was one of the biggest outbreaks in history. The strangest thing happened. An art dealer in Boston was watching the coverage on tv when he saw a barn on the outside of Maple Creek that had been completely blown away. The reporter pointed out that although the damage to the buildings was horrendous, a scarecrow standing in the vegetable garden was unscathed. The art dealer was a very accomplished collector and he recognized immediately that it was part of the ISG heist. He called the Carroll County Sheriff's Office and reported he had seen a rare Roman Galea in the video, and he thought it was a stolen artifact."

"That's a strange story, alright, but what's that got to do with me?"

"I was just wondering why you would put a $350,000 helmet on a scarecrow's head!" Ford said, almost laughing.

"Your curiosity is a little bit underdeveloped. This happened in 1999, and you're just now asking me about it? That's strange to me." Casey said.

"The Carroll County Sheriff was covered up with emergency calls, and recovery efforts, so he sent a parttime auxiliary officer out to check it out. The officer took the galea back to the police station and left it in a junk room at the jail. It was there until about a year ago. They've been using it as a hat rack. The art dealer died five days after making the report. He was taking a dirt nap, so it wasn't a concern to him after that."

"That still doesn't explain what that has to do with me," Casey said.

"We've got a rookie who's also a storm freak. He watches all these old storm videos. We've got him reviewing closed case files, and old unsolved high-profile crimes. He was reading your case file after staying up half the night watching the Weather Channel special on tornados. He saw the scarecrow and remembered the ancient helmet when he was going through the ISG files. He did a little follow up and the next thing we knew, Agent Green and I were in Maple Creek, Oklahoma putting two and two together. Since you're a lawyer, we checked the court files for anything with your name on it. Lo and behold, you did a land deal for a Chicago real estate developer back in 1995 right there in the Carroll County Courthouse. With a little leg work we found Savanah Anderson, still living on the farm."

"And she said she knew me?"

"No, she said she didn't know you. But I thought she

was a little evasive when I showed her the sketch."

"Then, again, what's this helmet got to do with me?"

Ford took his hands out of his pockets and walked to Casey's desk. He picked up the sketch, "she said she didn't know you, but we located the mail carrier who is still alive and still carrying the mail. He said there was a guy hanging around Savanah Anderson's farm during that time, and strangely, he said they guy looked a lot like this sketch."

"Like I said, Agent Ford. There are only so many faces in the world to go around."

Agent Green stepped away from the window. He put both hands in his pockets, looking down at Casey, he cleared his throat. Casey laughed. "You guys have a tell. Every time you get ready to make a play, you stick both your hands into your pockets. Not a good habit for a gambler, and that's pretty much been your game up until now," Casey said.

Green ignored the remark. "You must have been all out of options when you stuck that $300,000 galea on that scarecrow's head," Green said, snorting softly. Casey shrugged and smiled.

"You would have been carrying that thing around with you for five years. It was probably rolling around in the trunk of your car screaming, I'm worth a lot of money, Casey!" Green said light heartedly.

"The love of money is the root of all evil, Tyrese." Casey said.

"We've had a few setbacks on this case, Casey, but we're closing in on you. It's just a matter of time," Ford said, again taking the lead.

Casey wanted to explore what Ford and Green had found. It didn't matter at this point, but he was curious.

He was proud of the fact he could fly a helicopter, and that Terry Smith had taught him how to do it. Ford and Green had never hit on how they had obtained the sketch they depended upon so heavily. He knew how they got it, but it would never hold up in court. It was all about the helicopter, and their secret witness.

The helicopter had a story of its own. In 1989 the Berlin wall was toppled, and the Soviet Union was on the ash heap of history. A group of college kids at Sangamon State University in anticipation of the fall had organized a celebration on the steps of the state capitol. When the people behind the iron curtain started pouring through the opening it was live on tv and radio. Most people in American knew what was happening and many were celebrating. Fireworks and loud chanting began on the Capitol lawn at 3:00 am. There were three hundred people there and the streets all around it were jammed with cars honking and lights flashing. Squad cars were stationed at South Second Street and Lawrence, and Second Street and Monroe with red and blue lights oscillating. A quiet clicking sound was approaching in the air just over the Illinois Supreme Court building, but nobody noticed until an OH Cayuse 6 helicopter dropped nearly to street level and then shot upward. It narrowly missed the heavy utility lines on Adams Street and then tilted sideways. The people on the State Capitol lawn later said they could hear someone shouting, God bless America, as an arm was waving an American flag outside the pilot's window. The copter circled the Capitol dome and buzzed the police station. It continued to fly erratically around the downtown area until a Blackhawk copter from the National Guard depot arrived and escorted it to Sacred Heart Griffin high school baseball field where it was forced to land.

Casey caught the case on Monday morning at the circuit clerk's office where cases on the indigent list were assigned by the Public Defender. He was reviewing the file while being escorted to the cell block in the Sangamon County Jail. He smiled as he read. What the hell, he thought to himself.

He found his client in a cell with steel bars and a cot against the wall. There was a new modern county jail under construction, but the current jail resembled Statesville Prison. His client's name was Gabriel Stevenson. He was sitting on his cot with his chin resting in his palms. Casey approached the cell and called out, "Mr. Stevenson."

Stevenson got up and walked to the bars and grasp one with each hand. "You can call me Gabby. Everybody else does," he said, turning his head and directing his remark down the cell block.

"You got that right!" Someone shouted.

"Another voice said, "he just stopped talking a minute ago. He talked all night long!"

Casey chuckled. His client was standing there with his fist clutching the bars, his beard was bristling, his hair was standing on ends, and huge blue eyes were glistening like a kid who was about to get candied up. He laughed when he heard another voice from the distance say, "You talk too much, Gabby."

"You seem happy for a guy who just got arrested for buzzing the state capitol," Casey said.

"I was celebrating," Gabby said.

"I saw it on the news," Casey said. "I think we can get you in front of a judge this morning and get you out of here."

"Look at me. I'm not ready to go before a judge." He held his hands out with his palms up. He was wearing brown bib Carhart overalls with tiny round holes, and grease stains all over them. A broken front tooth didn't help his appearance.

"I've seen worse," Casey said.

As they walked down the hallway towards the elevator to the courtrooms on the third floor, escorted by a deputy sheriff, Casey asked Gabby where he got the helicopter. "I bought it at the army surplus depot in East Saint Louis. I could have bought a tank too, but I didn't know how to get it home."

"You can afford a helicopter and a tank, but you can't afford an attorney," Casey hmphed.

"I bought it for a hundred dollars. It was junk. I overhauled the engine and replaced one of the blades. If I didn't buy it, they would have crushed it and sold it for scrap metal. I saved the old girl."

"Do you have a pilot's license?"

"No. I had a military license but it expired a long time ago"

"Where'd you learn to fly?"

"I was in the army, stationed at Fort Leonard Wood. I took pilot training in a Huey. It's a little different but if you can fly a Huey, you can fly an OH-6 Cayuse."

"It's a lot smaller," Casey said.

"Quieter too. I flew all over my property and nobody ever took notice. You know if it was noisy people would have been calling the police all the time. Somehow everybody thinks when they see a copter or plane along the tree line, it's about to crash."

"Well, whatever," Casey said as they entered the

courtroom.

The judge was accustomed to seeing Casey in his courtroom with a defendant who couldn't afford bail. He knew Casey would be asking for Gabby to be released on his own recognizance. He trusted Casey's judgement, so it was only a matter of minutes before Gabby was released. Casey drove Gabby home. He lived in Auburn Illinois, a few miles south of Springfield. It was a junk yard. The lane was lined with rusty cars, broken down farm equipment and junk of all kinds.

"Where's your copter?" Casey asked.

"I think it's out behind my office. I signed a release for a National Guard pilot to fly it home. They didn't have a place to keep it at the depot."

"I've never heard of anything like that," Casey said with astonishment.

The long driveway to the office was caked with motor oil, littered with car mufflers, crumpled fenders, and old tires. When they arrived at the office Gabby stood in front of a little shack with broken windows, and roofing shingles hanging over the ledge. "This is where it all happens," Gabby said, extending both arms, smiling broadly through his broken teeth. He was as skinny as a number two pencil. He looked like a scarecrow standing there with his hair on ends and a wiry red beard bristling.

They walked around back and found the OH-6 sitting between two junk corvettes. Gabby cranked up the copter, and they took a spin around the property. Gabby landed and Casey took his turn with the stick. It was quiet and handled like a dream. "The engine sounds great," Casey said.

"When you run a junk business you learn how to work on things," Gabby said.

They zipped around the property and the fields close by. Casey was wearing a smile the entire time. He thought about Vietnam, and Terry Smith. He never thought he would ever have another chance to operate a helicopter, but here he was, flying high with a scarecrow as his passenger.

Casey represented Gabby throughout his trial and was able to get a sentence of one year court supervision. The judge was amused by Gabby, but several times he had to tell him that he couldn't just talk whenever he felt the urge. It was a comedy. When Gabby left the courtroom the judge said, "Ah, Gabby. Don't buzz the capitol again." Both Casey and Gabby turned and smiled.

When they parted Gabby told Casey that anytime he wanted to borrow the copter, he was welcome to it. Now in his little boat office in Wisconsin, he was curious about the FBI, and what they knew about a helicopter being involved in the ISG heist. They had never given him the details, other than suggesting that he might have learned how to fly from Terry Smith.

Now both Ford and Green were up wandering around the office. Green was checking each window to gauge the depth of snow on all sides of the building. When he got to the rear window he noticed a toilet stool in the corner, a sink and a ventilation pipe from the concrete floor to the ceiling. "You don't get much privacy around here, do you Casey?" He said, standing beside the toilet stool with his hand resting against the vent pipe. Casey held his breath hoping the pipe didn't fold in the middle where it had been spliced.

"There's a curtain you can slide over if you have to use the facilities, Tyrese."

"No, just admiring the décor," Green said facetiously.

Casey realized he had a concerned expression on his face and hoped Ford hadn't noticed. Ford was looking at him but didn't seem to question it. Casey's office had been searched by a forensic team on two occasions, but Casey wasn't there for either event. He couldn't believe they had missed that the ventilation pipe was not as secure as it should have been. But who would think it had anything to do with a 500-million-dollar theft?

"I'm an attorney. In addition to being interrogated every few years, I'm familiar with how these things go, Lee. You have to give up a little information to make progress," Casey said.

"We're all friends here, Casey, what do you wanna know?"

"You're interested in me knowing how to fly a copter, why is that? I'm just curious about that. I don't have a license to fly. I heard a rumor about something you've never released to the public."

"What's that, Casey?"

"There was a secret witness to something that happened at the same time the robbery was going down. Somebody saw something unusual in the amphitheater near the museum. I heard it was something to do with an object from the sky and that sketch."

"It was a helicopter, Casey. You know that, and you're too smart to think that we don't know that you know it. So why don't you tell us about it?"

Casey knew it, but he wasn't going to admit it. He

smiled without answering. Ford thought he was getting close to bringing everything down on Casey's head or he wouldn't be giving up such a crucial piece of information. There are things in life when you can remember every detail about it. Bob Gibson could remember every pitch he made during the 1968 World Series, and that wasn't nearly as consequential as perpetrating a 500-million-dollar theft. Casey could remember every minute of that flight into the grounds of that little amphitheater on March 15th, 1990.

He transported the OH-6 from Auburn, Illinois to Worchester, Massachusetts on a flatbed trailer. Gabby had painted it black at Casey's request, and the blades had been removed for transportation. It was secured with cables and chains and covered with tarp. It was impossible to identify it as a copter traveling down the highway. He had researched the area thoroughly and knew it was one of the most wooded areas in the state. There was a farm property that had been in dispute between heirs of deceased parents, a bank holding the deed, and a savings and loan with a second mortgage. It had been unoccupied for five years without upkeep. There were a few pastures that hadn't completely grown up in new growth trees, but the rest of the land was wooded or covered with brush. Casey only needed one small piece of terra firma to launch. He had flown a Huey with Terry Smith in Vietnam, but he didn't know the requirements for flying in the United States. After doing a little research he was surprised to learn that most of the time it wasn't necessary to file a flight plan. There were news copters, crop dusters, and emergency copters operating all the time without one. That was good news to Casey. He could fly without air traffic control picking him up on radar and sending an interceptor after him. He remembered Gabby's assertion that people called the police all the time when airplanes and helicopters hovered too close to tree lines, believing they were in distress. When he launched, he wasn't going to waste time getting out of there. Metro West Emergency Care and Saint Vincent hospital were both directly in line between Worchester and Boston. They were both equipped with helipads. Helicopter traffic in that area wouldn't be unusual.

It was a week after Casey delivered the OH-6 to the field in Worchester that he rented a car from Hertz using a fake name and identification. He had the good luck of having a fabricated ID card in his files from a defendant he represented in a check writing scam. He used the car to scope out the entire area around ISG.

There was a lot of things swirling around in his mind when Agent Ford disclosed that they thought a copter had been involved in the heist, but Casey only reminisced about the flight and how that sketch had been procured. It was a story unto itself.

All the planning, and all the meetings and discussions about how they were going to rob that museum had fled the moment Casey lifted into the air from the field in Worchester. His only thought was to get to that landing site. He could see the lights on the ground in the woods. My God how many houses are there in the trees down there, he thought as he cruised at treetop level. During the daytime most of them were invisible from the road but now he thought he had never seen so many homes shrouded by the woods. The OH-6 could cruise at 150 miles per hour and turn on a dime. Gabby had done a good job of refurbishing that bird, and Casey had confidence in it. In Nam when he and Terry patrolled at night they watched for small arms gunfire from the blackness of the forest, but here he could see back porches, swimming pools, and headlight beams on the paved streets below. It was so different watching all of that disappearing beneath the nose of the OH-1 as he powered through the rural areas, and outlying neighborhoods of Worchester.

He kept his eye on his watch knowing he would have to be precise on timing. He had the bag phone in the seat, ready to make the call telling the others he was in position. Being aloft in his little flying grasshopper strangely evoked memories from his past life. There was that fluttering in his stomach meandering through his mind and his body. Moving around from one little town to another, shoveling pig shit in a sale barn, fighting and killing people in a war he didn't understand, all of that was present in his thoughts. He thought about his high school girlfriend dumping him. It was all there fluttering away in waves as he sped along in the sky. I guess that's just who I am, he thought.

It was exactly 1:10 am when Casey arrived over the college campus. A Mardi Gras celebration was going on in the grass in front of the library of Saint Thomas College. There was already a news helicopter in the air filming the activity on the ground. He could see the museum, and two police officers on a golf cart on the bicycle trail near the Mardi Gras celebration. The OH-6 was quiet and dark against the sky. The amphitheater was empty, and barely visible in the woods but for one utility light near the stage. As he was hovering at tree level preparing to land, he saw a figure running along a pathway through the woods. It was a seventeen-year-old Evie Rainforth. She was drunk and high on mescaline, a hallucinogenic drug. When she saw the helicopter settling in the grass she was frozen in her tracks. She tilted backwards and fainted, falling with a thud, her head hitting the ground hard. At that point Casey had already called the others telling them he was in position.

"Fuck!" Casey grunted. What do I do now? He thought.

Against his better judgement, Casey jumped out of the OH-6 and ran to the girl. She had vomited and was aspirating. The gurgling sound coming from her throat signaled that she was in real trouble. He rolled her to her side and cleared the vomit from her mouth. She wasn't breathing! He pounded her back and a stream of yellow liquid shot onto the ground. He put his ear to her mouth and listened. It was silent. He cupped his hand over her nose, covered her lips with his mouth and breathed in. After five breaths she coughed and opened her eyes. She wasn't startled. She gazed at Casey as if in a dream.

Casey got her to her feet and walked her through the woods. It was 1:30 am by that time. His partners were surely inside the museum. He hurriedly placed Evie on a park bench on the bicycle path. A group of revelers dressed in Mardi Gras outfits were walking toward them, laughing and making a lot of noise. Casey ran back through the woods.

Evie was found semi-conscious and transported to Metro West Emergency Care. After being admitted under those circumstances the police were called to make an incident report. A uniformed officer of the

Boston Police Department talked to Evie, hoping to learn where she had acquired the drugs, and to get an explanation of what happened. She was serious when she told the officer she had seen an unidentified flying object. An earthling like creature had confronted her and groped her at the college amphitheater. She was breathless as she explained how she floated on air out of the woods and to safety.

The officer laughed, filed his report and went back on patrol. By then Casey was on his way back to Springfield, Illinois. Boston detectives were hard at work trying to run down clues to the biggest heist in American history.

The ISG Museum had been robbed of 500 million in irreplaceable art. They didn't follow up on the incident report until several days later. The importance of Evie's encounter had been temporarily lost.

Chapter Eleven

The wind had died down, and now the largest snowflakes ever seen were falling straight in a white curtain, covering the ground like a thick white blanket. The frustration on Agent Green's face was easy to read. Agent Ford disregarded it.

"Casey, we know there was a helicopter involved in the heist. The Boston PD received calls of a helicopter circling on campus grounds at 1:00 am on March 15th. You already know that was the time the robbery got under way. We have a witness who saw you. That's where we got the sketch."

"Really, there were rumors that your witness thought your helicopter was a UFO, Lee. How will that all stand up in court?"

"Casey, that's information we've never let out in public. There's no way you would know anything about our witness unless you were there. You know you don't have to say anything, right?" Ford said.

"Right," Casey said.

"Being an attorney, you know you have a right to talk to one of your fellow attorneys, don't you? A right to remain silent.?"

"I learned that the first day of law school."

"You can call one of them anytime you want, maybe on the phone, right?"

"Right," Casey chuckled.

"If you get tired of listening to me asking these stupid questions you can tell me to fuck off, don't you,

Casey?"

"I do. I know that Lee, but I'm amused."

"If you make a confession, or give me information that might cause me to file for an arrest warrant, I can tell the judge about our conversation in a criminal trial against you, right?"

"Yes, Lee, I know that. It sounds like you just read me my Miranda Warnings, and I gotta say, it was quite unique," Casey said, smiling. "Are you going to arrest me?

"No, but I'm going to ask you some direct questions."

"Shoot," Casey said.

"How did you know our witness reported your copter as a UFO?"

"I heard it through the grapevine, Lee. Cops talk. Maybe every guy on duty that night got the skinny on a drugged teenager reporting a UFO. That's hard info to keep under wraps. She gave your sketch artist a description of a guy you say who looks like me. Do I look like I'm from another planet to you?"

"You know what you just said is evidence, don't you Casey? You have information about a witness we've kept under wraps for thirty years. That's strong circumstantial evidence. Why don't you go ahead and give us the details, and give the names of the others?"

"I even heard that it was several days before the detectives questioned her about what happened to her. She still thought she had been groped by an alien who looked like that drawing," Casey said laughing out loud. "Lee, do you know how that sounds?"

"She's a viable witness, Casey. They realized this girl was traumatized by running into you in the dark.

When they put two and two together, it added up. When they gave it to us, we reviewed everything, and we made you a long time ago. We just didn't have enough to put the irons on you. I think this thing with the Roman galea is the topping on the cake."

"It may be just that, Lee, but I'm betting this case will never go to court. Am I under arrest?"

Ford looked at Casey with a different expression now. It wasn't anger, but it was easy to see he was suppressing his frustration. "Am I under arrest?" Casey asked again. Ford was quiet. "I didn't think so," Casey said.

Ford walked to the window and looked out. "You're right, Tyrese. We better get out of here before we're stuck."

"You're stuck now. There's six inches of snow out there and this lane is sixty feet long," Casey said. Both of them looked at Casey like he had deliberately trapped them there in the wilderness.

As Casey predicted Agent Ford and Green's car was immobile. Casey watched out the window as Ford rocked the car back and forth trying to get it to move. Casey slipped into his Carhart overalls, his rubber boots, and a floppy eared winter hat and left the office by the back door. When he appeared around in front of the office his Troy-Bilt heavy duty snow blower was pumping snow into the air with a vengeance. Casey smiled when he made his first pass near the Agent's car. The overalls and the Cousin Eddy winter hat was proof he was at home in the Wisconsin outback. Agent Ford chuckled at the sight.

The snow continued to fall but it was no match for the monstrous snow blower. Within minutes the sixty-foot lane was clear and negotiable. When the job was done Casey walked to Ford's car window. Ford rolled it down. Casey rested his arms on the door panel and looked in.

"The hard road will be clear. These road crews in Wisconsin can work miracles."

"Thank you, Casey," Ford said pleasantly.

"Not necessary, I had to get out anyway."

Ford was silent for a moment before he spoke. "Casey, you need to get a lawyer."

"I am a lawyer," he said.

"An attorney who represents himself has a fool for a client," Green interjected from the far side of the car.

"We'll see," Casey said. "See you later."

Chapter Twelve

Jake Brenner had little to do with the ISG heist, but he had been a thorn in Casey's side for twenty-five years. Casey understood why, but it was still irritating. Jake didn't put anything on the line, but he wanted his share. Casey had warned Jake on numerous occasions not to call him, but he did anyway. FBI agents were constantly monitoring his activity, and they were never going to lose interest in him. There was five hundred million dollars involved and it would always be a priority.

In the beginning when Casey approached Brenner in 1990, he was working as a human resource manager at Benders Department Stores in Kewanee, Illinois. He was little more than a flunky for the store manager, in debt, paying a mortgage for his ex-wife, and child support for a daughter who wouldn't give him the time of day. Casey had sympathy for the man, but he always knew Brenner would never amount to anything. He believed Brenner was so much a coward that if he approached him with the proposal, he would either shrink away like a scared dog or accept the offer and stay as little involved as possible. Going to the police about Casey's offer would never cross his mind. Casey knew that and believed Brenner would at least consider it. His bet was that Brenner would jump in with both feet.

When Casey found Brenner, he was living in an apartment over a junk store on Main Steet in the downtown portion of the town. Kewanee was a little over ten thousand people, so finding him wasn't much of a task. Inside the front door of the building Where the store was located was a metal suit of armor standing, leaning forward with a sign in its hand stating, WELCOME. It looked more like the Tin Man in the Wizard of Oz than a medieval warrior. An older man was leaning with both elbows planted on the counter with cigar smoke circling his head. He greeted Casey with as much interest as a cat looking at lettuce in his feeding bowl. When Casey asked about Brenner, he explained that Brenner lived aloft and directed him to the back entrance where two levels of shaky stairs led to his apartment. Casey could see through the window, Brenner sitting in an overstuffed chair with a beer can in his hand, and two empties lying on the floor in front of him. He knocked and Brenner jumped as if startled. When he came to the door, he stared out the glass wide eyed like a man waiting to be cracked in the head with a hammer. When he finally recognized Casey, he nearly took the door off its hinges getting it open.

"Casey!" he exclaimed, reaching for him with both hands.

Casey chuckled.

"What the hell are you doing here?"

"I need to talk, Jake. Maybe I can come inside?"

Brenner turned slightly, looking at the interior of his apartment. "It's a mess, Casey." And it truly was a mess. The brown carpeting was matted from spills, the walls were dingy, and dirty clothes were strewn all over the place.

"It's okay, Jake. I live alone. I know how it is."

Casey stepped inside as Brenner led the way to a tiny kitchen with a table and two chairs. Brenner cleaned off the paper plates and crumbs before sitting down. "How about a beer, Casey?"

"Sure."

Brenner fetched two Stag beers from a tiny refrigerator and popped the tops. It was uneasy for a moment as Casey tried not to look around. Jake continued to apologize for the surroundings. Casey contemplated how he was going to make his proposal without sounding like he had lost his mind. Finally, he said, "Jake, what was it like when you were a security guard at the ISG Museum in Boston?"

Brenner's expression was like he had been asked if he wanted a free ticket to the Super Bowl. "Are you going to rob it!" He exclaimed.

"Why would you ask something like that?" Casey asked, completely shocked by Brenner's response.

Brenner laughed, and snorted, covering his mouth. "I don't know! Are you?" He gasped.

When Casey said, yes, Brenner jumped out of his chair, giggling like an idiot. "I knew it! I've been thinking about robbing that place for ten years. I've thought about the way you were interested in it back when we were in Nam! Every time I envisioned it, I always thought of you."

From that point forward, it wasn't a matter of whether you would be on board, but, when and how will we do it.

In the weeks to come, Casey financed a trip to Boston where they visited the Museum. They were careful about their clothing, and constantly cognizant of security cameras. Brenner was surprised at how little the place had changed. Once Casey was familiarized with the security, and the museum layout, Brenner's involvement was finished. There was no way Casey would trust Shaky Jake to be sturdy enough to be involved in the robbery. Still, he promised Brenner full partnership in the loot.

Thirty years later, Brenner was still waiting for his part of the take. The money had never been a motivation for Casey, and he had been naïve to think he could find an outlet for five hundred million dollars' worth of stolen art. He didn't have any idea where a buyer could be found, and he neglected to research it. As stupid as it was, he had done just as Agent Ford and Green accused him of doing. He robbed the ISG Museum to even the score for Jason Keys. Casey was thirty-five years old when the ISG Museum heist went down, and now he was seventy-four. Brenner had been hounding him for money ever since, and in all fairness, it wasn't unreasonable.

April 1st, 1995, twenty-five years before Agent Ford and Agent Green showed up at Casey's little boat office. Brenner made a move that was risky at best. Casey was in the Motorola Store on South Sixth Street in Springfield, Illinois trading in his bag phone for a handheld flip phone. He had 500 million dollars' worth of art treasures hidden in a little cabin he was using in Lake Waubesa, Wisconsin, but since it wasn't generating income, he was still working out of his car in Springfield, Illinois. Everybody involved in the ISG heist were anxious for a return on their involvement, but they thought it is what it is, and all but Brenner were patient. Brenner was chomping at the bit to get rich. Casey was never surprised when Brenner called for an update, or to make some stupid proposal for selling the goods.

The new phone was assigned the same number as Casey's bag phone, so it was ready to go the moment Casey paid the bill and signed the three-year contract. Before he got out of the store his new cell was ringing. It took him a few seconds to find the accept button. "Hello," he said.

"It's me."

Casey exhaled. "Yeah, Jake, what now?" He was irritated, but at the same time, he felt guilty that he didn't have anything new to tell him.

"I'm in Charleston, North Carolina."

"What are you doing there?"

"I got a lead on an art dealer. He deals in stolen stuff, and I've got an appointment with him. I told him I've got the stuff from ISG Museum."

"God damnit! Jake, it's probably a trap! The FBI runs stings like that all the time!"

"Casey, it's all good, I got his name from Louie."

"Louie, who, for Christ's sake?"

"My landlord. Louie, the guy who owns the junk store downstairs."

"What did you tell Louie, Jake. Did you say anything about the heist?"

"No, I didn't Casey. I didn't say anything about it at all. Louie was telling me all about this guy who came all the way from North Carolina to look at a painting he posted on the internet. Do you know what that is, the internet?"

"Yes, I know what it is, but get on with it."

"The painting was a replica of a valuable piece of art that's been missing for a long time. The Nazi's stole it, or something like that. He came all the way from North Carolina to look at it. He used a loupe to examine it, but he knew it was fake even before he did that."

"How did you get his name and address – his phone number?"

"I took it off of Louie's notes when he wasn't there."

"You didn't call him from your phone, did you?

"No, Casey, I'm not stupid. I drove out here and called him from a pay phone. He said we need to talk about it. I didn't even tell him what we have. I just said the ISG Museum stuff."

"Call him and tell him you need three days to get things together before you can meet him. I'm coming out there."

Casey packed an overnight bag and headed for Lake Waubesa, Wisconsin. It was a seven-hour drive to the little cabin on the lake that he owned. It was a boat shop he bought from a guy who had gone broke repairing boats and selling used parts. Casey called it his office for tax purposes. The sun was already gone when Casey drove down the backroads to his destination. He wanted to make quick work of his detail there and get back on the road. He cursed under his breath thinking about Brenner throwing a monkey wrench into the mix. He wasn't prepared for this crap, but he had to deal with it.

The moon was visible through the trees and the white light was glittering on the lake. It was a beautiful evening, but Casey wasn't there to enjoy the surroundings. He parked the car and hurried inside. He took out a Sears Sawzall, a Polaroid camera, and a three-inch pipe connector from a canvass bag he had brought with him. A toilet stool in the corner was standing completely open to the world without walls, or anything to provide privacy. Casey plugged the Sawzall into the outlet and hit the switch. The blade went into motion as Casey approached the three-inch ventilation pipe beside the toilet stool. Cutting through the pvc pipe was like a hot knife going through butter. When Casey separated the top section from the bottom, million-dollar paintings wrapped in cellophane started falling out like water from a facet. It took a few minutes to peel off the cellophane and lay the paintings out on a table. Casey took his time to photograph each painting with the polaroid, being as steady as possible to get a clear print. When he was finished, he rolled each of them up, wrapped them again in cellophane and stuck them back into the pipe. He applied glue to the connecter and stuck the pipe back together. He sat down in a chair and looked at his handywork. "There, good as new!" he said aloud.

He didn't take long to admire his work before he was back on the road. It was a fourteen-hour drive from Wisconsin to Charleston. He stopped and slept at a Motel Six in Mercer County West Virginia. It was a rough night. A construction crew was rowdy in the parking lot until the early hours of the morning. When he left, he saw them loading up their gear in slow motion.

When Casey arrived in Charleston, Brenner was waiting at the Tar Heels Café on Bradford Street. He found a parking spot at the curb within walking distance. When he entered Brenner was sitting in a booth across from the counter. Casey was tired and the lines on his face had deepened during the last seventy-two hours. Brenner watched him walking to his booth, trying to get a read on his state of mind. His eyes were focused on Brenner like a hungry hawk eyeing a snake in the grass. Casey slid into the seat across from Brenner without saying anything, but his expression said it all.

"I'm glad you're here, Casey. We really need to get things moving."

"You don't have a clue, do you Brenner," Casey said gruffly.

"Casey, it's been nearly five years since we robbed that museum. Nobody has seen a dime of the money."

Brenner's remark stuck in Casey's craw, and he bit down grinding his teeth, the muscles in his jaws were twitching. "Jake, remind me how we robbed that museum, and what you did?" Casey said. He was conflicted about the situation. Brenner and the others had the right to be anxious, and demanding, but there was just no easy way to unload that stuff. Brenner didn't put anything on the line outside of touring the place and educating Casey on the security system. He understood Brenner's frustration, but he resented it too. He really didn't deserve a full share, but a fourth of nothing is nothing.

"I'm trying to help." Brenner said.

Casey exhaled. "I know you are, but you don't know how these things work. The FBI is never going to give up on this case. There is a 500-million-dollar value on the stuff we stole. I've discreetly worked to find someone to broker it, but there's nobody out there who can help. The Feds run stings to draw people in. I'm afraid this might just be the case here."

"Maybe this guy can get us a deal. I'm going to meet him and see what he thinks," Brenner said defiantly.

"No, you're not. You'll screw it up and we'll all end up in jail. I'll talk to him," Casey stated sternly. "Okay, that's fine, but I need money, Casey."

They were both quiet. Casey exhaled, staring at Brenner with an annoyed expression. He recalled basic training when Brenner fainted straight away. He didn't have any substance whatsoever. The odds of him doing something like robbing the ISG Museum without Casey to lean on was as likely as flying monkeys attacking the pentagon. Casey knew that and he was ashamed of his resentment. But he couldn't help but wanting to choke him until his eyeballs popped out.

"Jake, you sit tight. I'll talk to this guy. If we can get something going, we will."

An hour later Casey was entering a small art store on West Morehead Street. The paintings hanging on the walls and sitting on easels didn't look any less distinguished than those he had stuffed in the vent pipe in his boat shop office.

It was quiet. There were no customers. Mozart was playing softly in the background. There was a fluttering sensation in Casey's stomach as he waited, not knowing what to expect. Was this a trap? The door opened from the back room and a short chubby man came out. He glanced at his watch. His glasses on the tip of his nose, receding hairline, and dark bushy eyebrows were reminiscent of Mr. Whipple in the Charmin toilet tissue commercials.

"Are you interested in anything in particular?" he asked.

"Rembrandt, maybe," Casey said.

Mr. Whipple was looking over his glasses with an uneasy expression in his eyes. "Have you ever heard the term, entrapment, sir?

Casey smiled, "I have but I'm not a cop."

"Did you call me looking for something for Louie? He asked.

"I did," Casey said.

"Your voice is different."

"My client called."

"Well then, lets step into my office."

Mr. Whipple didn't waste any time. As soon as the door was shut, he asked, "What have you got?"

Casey didn't say a word. He reached into his pocket and retrieved the polaroid pictures he had taken. Mr. Whipple laid them out under a goose neck magnifying loupe. He looked at each photograph for several seconds. "I thought your client was lying about this, but Holy Mother of God, this is the real deal!"

"Can we talk about a deal?" Casey asked.

"Actually, I thought you might have some authentic looking copies I might broker for you, but this is over my head. I've done some deals on stolen art the Nazis robbed from the Jews, but this is scary. This is way too risky for me. I can keep my eyes open for maybe another dealer, but no. This isn't for me."

Casey gathered up his polaroid's and stuck them into his pocket. As Casey opened the door to the street, the Mr. Whipple look alike said, "How do I contact you if I hear something?"

"You don't," Casey said.

Several days later, Mr. Whipple was arrested by the Charleston Police Department for possession of stolen American Indian artifacts. He tried to work a deal with the prosecutor for information regarding the ISG Museum robbery. FBI agents were called in and he identified the police sketch they had fashioned from the description given to them by Evie Rainforth. That was the day Casey became an FBI person of interest. During the cabin interview it had been mentioned. Even at the time he had encountered Mr. Whipple, he knew there would be a time in the future when this meeting would come up. It came up numerous times in the years that followed.

Chapter Thirteen

Jason Keys was unjustly fired for Conduct Unbecoming a Police Officer. His wife divorced him a year later. Casey stayed in contact with Jason after he represented him in the civil service hearing. They became friends, and as bizarre as it was, they robbed the ISG Museum. The most peculiar choice for partners in crime were Shaky Jake Brenner, and a little troll like guy by the name of Billy Willey.

There are some things in life that just stink. Jason Keys was a good cop. If any run of the mill drunk had rampaged through that intersection at Ninth and North Grand other than Dean Allen Marlo, it would have been a routine DUI and Reckless Driving arrest. Marlo ruined Jason's life. The only job he could get in law enforcement was as Chief of Police in Virden, Illinois, a town of twenty-five hundred people. Casey had some liberal views about the legal justice system, but he was a staunch capitalist. The only thing he hated about capitalism was elitist like Dean Allen Marlo. When Jason was fired, it was a bitter pill to swallow. As crazy as it was, they robbed the ISG Museum because Casey thought Marlo needed a comeuppance, and it was the biggest heist in American history. Getting rid of the loot was a much greater task than doing the crime. But still there was satisfaction in knowing they had put it right in Marlo's face.

After the incident with the Mr. Whipple art dealer, Casey was discreet about having contact with the others. Casey was still in the habit of reading everything he could get his hands on so when he read that Mr. Whipple had been arrested, he knew he would try to make a deal. Guys like Mr. Whipple usually squealed like pigs when they were caught. Face recognition technology was pioneered in the 1960's and by 1995 it was a routine tool for the FBI. If they hadn't identified Casey from the Evie Rainforth sketch it would have been highly unlikely. Investigating every person in Casey's life would be a routine matter after that.

Casey left Charleston as uneasy as a man with a bone stuck in his throat. Brenner worried him. The earth would turn sideways and do flips through the universe before Brenner would confess to robbing ISGM, but he didn't have enough self-discipline to control his eagerness to get a little jingle in his pocket. Casey warned him that prison was an atrocious place for a fair-skinned light-haired guy like himself. Brenner swore to God he would never do anything like that again.

It was a long trip back to Springfield. Casey listened to tapes he had made in reference to a few cases he had on the docket. There never was a bigger hypocrite than Casey. He was conscientious about serving his clients and maintaining his integrity in the Justice system. How could that be possible? The perpetrator of the largest robbery in American history going about his civic duties. It was funny too. They were the gang who couldn't shoot straight that had done it. That was all on his mind as he drove through the mountains back to Illinois.

When Casey learned that Mr. Whipple had been

arrested, he drove the short distance to Virden where he found Jason Keys sitting in his squad car on an abandoned service station drive. When he pulled up next to Jason, he rolled his window down. Jason pitched the magazine he was reading into the passenger seat of his squad car.

"What's going on, Jason?"

"Just being vigilant against criminal behavior here in Virden," Jason laughed.

"You're doing it. It's quiet here on the mean streets."

"I could get a complaint about a barking dog, or maybe something as crucial as a garbage fire at any minute."

Casey looked down the street. There was a guy walking his dog, and another man raking the leaves in his front yard. He tightened his lips and bit down on the worry churning in his mind. "We need to get together, Jason. I've spent some time putting out a fire. Maybe we can have a few beers and talk. I'd like for Billy to be there, too."

"What about Brenner?"

"He's the reason we need to talk," Casey said,

"I'm free unless the mayor calls wanting me to do an emergency inspection at the trailer court, or to file a dog bite report," Jason said facetiously.

Casey laughed. "I'll see you at Mickeys in Springfield tomorrow night. I've got cases this afternoon, so I gotta head," he said as he rolled up the window to leave.

It was a gloomy afternoon, and a faint mist permeated the air. It was fifty degrees, but it felt wet and cold. When Casey walked into Mickeys. The neon lights, and dangling beer signs did little to illuminate the bar, it was dark and inauspicious. Billy was already there with a cola sitting on the table in front of him. Casey immediately felt better. The smile on Billy's face was like finding a gas station in the desert when you were running on empty. "There's my friend, and my attorney, Casey Rakestraw!"

"Hey, Billy."

"Jason called me, he'll be here in a few," Billy said.

Just at that moment Jason was walking through the door. He raised his hand and said, "Helen, I'll have a Budweiser, and get whatever they're having," he said, pointing at Casey and Billy.

"Billy is good, and I think Casey takes a Blue Moon," she said, watching Casey waiting for his nod. "Yep," Casey said, giving her a thumbs up.

They talked and laughed it up for a while, but finally Jason said, "What kind of fires have you been dealing with, Casey?"

Casey glanced around, carefully checking the distance between them and other customers. "It's Brenner, he wants money, and I don't blame him. But he did something stupid, and I got caught up in it."

Jason looked concerned, but Billy didn't seem to care at all. He believed Casey walked on water. He was able to get Billy a job at the courthouse filing case records in the Circuit Clerk's Office and had his conviction for disorderly conduct expunged. Billy had never been happier in his life, and it was all because of Casey. He thought Casey could handle anything.

"Brenner is a fucked-up dude," Jason said. Casey laughed. Jason had never met Brenner, but through Casey, Jason had formed an opinion of him, and he got it right.

"I've got to say this, and I know I've said it before, but I'm sorry about everything. I got you guys into this, and I didn't have any idea how we could broker that stuff."

Billy interrupted, "Your smart, Casey, you'll figure it out." His squeaky high-pitched voice was music to Casey's ears. The corners of Casey's lips turned up vaguely. What a loyal friend, he thought.

"Brenner contacted an art dealer in Charleston, North Carolina. He was getting ready to meet the guy and tell him about the stuff we have. I stopped him, but I had to meet the guy. He was a crook just like Brenner said, but he didn't want to touch the ISG Museum stuff. He wanted to contact me if he could find someone who would collaborate with us, but I didn't give him anything. It was a good thing too, because the FBI busted him last week for possession of stolen artifacts."

"Then, I guess we're all good," Jason said.

"Not really. I'm sure he's trying to wrangle a deal with them. He'll be going through mug shots and looking at the police sketch they ran in the papers back then. Once they identify me, they'll be looking at every case I've ever done, and everybody I know."

"If they've identified you, why don't they come after you?" Jason said. He was a sharp cop himself, and he knew that was pretty much routine.

'it's a sketch, Jason. Not a mug shot. The person in that sketch doesn't exist. It's a likeness. It won't stand up in court, but they'll use face recognition to match it to me, and probably some other guys too."

"So, what do you think?" Jason asked.

"They'll be watching us forever. They won't arrest

us because they want that stuff back. It's worth five hundred million dollars. They have to prove we have it. They won't move on us until they have it in their possession."

"It's scary, but I think we'll be okay," Jason said

"You guys will be alright. They don't have anything on you. Just don't give them anything if they pull you in for questioning."

"My lips are sealed," Billy said, zipping his thumb and forefinger across his mouth.

Garth Brooks was singing Friends in Low Places on the juke box. The tenor of the place had gradually slipped to a lower bearing as the conversation progressed. Casey knew that robbing the ISG Museum was stupid in the first place, but in retrospect it was more than that, it was insane.

Casey stared at his Blue Moon without making eye contact with the others. "I'm sorry I got you guys into this," he said.

Billy was still smiling, "Heck, Casey, it was the best time I ever had in my life!"

Casey looked at Billy. His face was lit up in the dim glow of the Budweiser sign. Casey chuckled at the absurdity of Billy's statement, and it made him feel better,

"I got to dress up in a police uniform, and ride in a helicopter. Jason and me got to hang out in a world-famous museum. It was fun, Casey," Billy said, taking his cola glass tapping it against Casey's Blue Moon bottle.

Jason leaned over and clicked his Budweiser against the top of Casey's bottle too. Jason said, "I did it for revenge, Casey. I wanted to kill Dean Allen Marlo. You kept me from being a murderer! The sonofabitch tried to destroy my life because I arrested him for drunken driving, he deserved to be shot. He's lucky we took him for five hundred million. I never even thought about the money"

"They were stupid to let us in, wasn't they, Jason? Have you ever seen a cop that looks like me?" Billy said loudly. Casey quickly looked around to see if he had attracted attention.

They quietly rehashed how they had planned the heist and described it to each other as if they had never heard it before. They rented a car in Springfield and drove to Worchester. The copter was there already. Casey purchased two throw away phones at Walmart for communication. It was new technology at the time, and at first it worried Casey, but they worked like a charm. There was a golf course next to the museum, and a park adjacent to that. Jason and Billy parked the car in the parking lot and rented a golf cart. When they got the word from Casey, Jason and Billy approached the employee door and demanded to be let in. It was as easy as that. The security guard let them in. When it was over, they took the golf cart to the amphitheater and made their getaway in the copter.

"Jason told me not to talk. He said my voice was so high pitched they'd think I was a girl. I didn't know my voice was high pitched, and besides that, ain't there no girl cops?" Billy said. Jason laughed. "You looked like Louie on Taxi dressed up in a police uniform."

Casey smiled, "When I set the copter down a drugged-up girl fainted and aspirated. I had to clean puke from her mouth and give her mouth-to-mouth resuscitation."

Billy giggled as Casey pretended to do heart depressions on the table. "Excuse me, honey, I have a robbery to get to."

Jason laughed out loud.

"When we took them boys to the basement and tied 'um up, Jason told 'em we were working for John Gotti, and if they gave the cops anything we were coming back with some wise guys to take care of business. It worked cause they didn't know nothin when it was all over."

They all chuckled softly. Casey looked around again to see if anyone was listening. "I'm afraid with what happened in Charleston, we're never going to unload that stuff," he said.

"I didn't do it for the money anyway, Casey," Jason said, reiterating what he had said earlier.

"Me, neither" Billy said. "I did it cause you're my friend, Casey."

Casey stared at the logo on his bottle. "I didn't do it for the money either," he said, "I don't know why I do anything. I jumped out of a helicopter on a bungee cord once. I don't know why I did that, but I liked it. Robbing that museum was the same thing. It was a hell of a jump for no reason," Casey said.

Jason reached over and clicked his bottle against Casey's Blue Moon bottle again. Billy did the same.

Casey still had the floor. "I decided to become a lawyer because I got hit with a horse turd. Explain that kind of logic. I hate lawyers. Most of them are bigger thieves than we are."

"You got that right," Jason said.

The bar was beginning to fill with the evening crowd. People were taking tables near them so talking

about the heist was finished. They had another beer,
promised each other to be cool about the situation, and
parted company.

Chapter Fourteen

When Casey met Jason and Billy at Mickey's Bar, it closed the door on finding a buyer for the art from the ISG Museum theft. Brenner was the only fly in the ointment, but Casey thought the warning he had given him about life behind bars might have put the fear of God into him. Brenner was an easy man to scare. He stopped contacting Casey after that. As time passed the promise of becoming a millionaire faded into the dust.

Casey was right about the face recognition capabilities of the Bureau. There were several faces that activated a hit, but Casey was the closest to being a duplicate. As a result, he became the FBI's number one person of interest. He was also right about the Bureau being reluctant to make a move without having a bead on the goods. That didn't mean they would give up on pinning him down. Several times over the next twenty years he was questioned, and it seemed endless. Ford and Green were just the most recent. During that time his car, his apartment, and his boat office in Wisconsin were searched. The paintings were in the ventilation pipe the entire time. Gabby's salvage yard had been the home of the Roman galea, resting in a pile of junk. Gabby died in 1994 so Casey picked it out of the pile and stuck it into his car trunk. It was there tumbling around for nearly a year before Casey decorated Savanah's scarecrow with it.

When Lee Ford advised Casey to get an attorney, it was the same as saying we're coming after you. Over the years the FBI had been tying the ends together. They had the sketch from Evie Rainforth and the fact he had represented Jason Keys solidly tied him to someone who had a grudge against Dean Allen Marlo. Having evidence that he knew how to fly a helicopter was clearly something they were going to use in court. They obviously believed a helicopter was used in the getaway, especially since there were several reports of a copter being in the air near the museum the night of the heist. Mr. Whipple had pinned Casey to the police sketch. Having a past affiliation with Shaky Jake Brenner was the topping on the cake. That was enough to present the case to a Grand Jury. Casey was concerned, but he had an ace up his sleeve. There was an escape route he had mulled over for years.

Casey's magnum snow blower got Agent's Ford and Green out of his lane in short order, but that didn't mean they would get back to the interstate. Casey left right after them and turned south in the same direction. When he arrived at the first stop sign, he found them in a ditch with snow all the way to the axels. Ford was behind the steering wheel, and Green was at the rear bumper with his shoulder against the trunk lid. Casey waved and smiled.

Something the agents had said motivated Casey to do something he had been struggling with. They talked about Savanah Anderson, and that prompted him to make his decision. He drove back to Springfield, Illinois, packed a bag and programed the GPS for Maple Creek, Oklahoma.

It was a long drive. He rolled into Maple Creek at 5:00 am. The lines on his face were deeper due to being on the road from Wisconsin, Illinois, and finally to

Maple Creek. He examined himself in the car mirror. An older man than he expected was looking back at him. Maybe some rest will help, He thought. He decided to check into the Maple Creek Motel to recuperate. He slept for six hours before rising to shower, and to cut and shave his beard. Looking at himself in the square mirror tiles that covered the entire wall, he wondered if Savanah would remember him. His weight was about the same, and his hair was thick, but white. He didn't have a mustache when he spent those two weeks with her in 1995. A trip back into the bathroom and his face was as slick as a baby's butt. He looked younger.

He drove the short distance to 1833 County Road Z. It was amazing that he remembered the address. When he arrived, Savanah was standing on the front porch in the same place she had waited for him in 1995. The tornado had done significant damage to the house and barn, but everything had been restored. She had long silver hair, and her body as trim as it had been the first time he saw her. Her face tan, free of makeup, and as smooth as a thirty-year-old's skin. Casey glanced at the mailbox at the gate. Savanah Anderson was printed in faded red letters. There was a scarecrow standing in the garden in the same place it had been when he left. A distinct glimmer of recognition was radiating from her eyes. The passive smile he remembered so well, had turned up the corners of her lips.

Opening the gate, Casey asked, "Do you know me?"

"Yes, I know you, Casey," she said.

"I was just passing through."

"Just passing through from Illinois, or some other place in the universe?"

"Illinois."

She didn't invite him to join her, but he took the three steps onto the porch. She waited a long moment, looking at him. It was the same gaze she had given him way back when. It was if she could see right into his very essence. A gaze so penetrating should have been unnerving, but instead warmth enveloped him. My God, he was instantly in love with her again.

"You're just in time to feed the chickens," she said.

"Okay," he said.

As they walked towards the shed to get the corn, Casey asked, "Is there a Mr. Anderson?

"Somewhere, but just not around here. My ex married the girl in town and that didn't last, and then he married a woman from Tulsa. The last time I heard anything about him he was divorced and living in Oklahoma City.

"You didn't, ah, get...."

"No, I live alone, Casey." She reached into the shed and retrieved a coffee can full of corn kernels. "Here," she said handing it to him. The chickens heard the shed door rattling and ran to him clucking and squawking, Casey pitched the corn into the air and watched the chickens scrambling for it.

"Did you come to sleep with me again, Casey?"

Casey smiled. She was so direct in everything she said, and that was liberating. Sleeping with her was always on his mind, even after fifteen years, but that was only part of it. He was never able to put his finger on what it was about her that swaddled him in emotion. She had been like a drug when he knew her before, and in this small dose, he was hooked again.

"Is that an invitation?" he asked.

"Of course, it is, but we have to feed the chickens."

The chickens got their corn, and bedtime came in the middle of the day. When they lie there together completely gratified physically, questions were niggling away at their thoughts. Casey was the first to ask. "You called me by my name. I thought we weren't using names. Wasn't my name supposed to be Simon?"

Savanah looked at the ceiling for a long moment. "The FBI told me your name," she said.

Casey wanted to ask how the conversation went, but he was silent. When she was ready to tell him about it, she would. He wasn't going to ask.

"They wanted to know where I got Freddy's helmet?"

"Freddy?"

"Freddy Kruger, my scarecrow."

"Oh, yeah, that," Casey said.

"I didn't know Freddy was wearing such expensive headgear. Agent Lee Ford said it was worth three hundred thousand dollars. That was kind of quaint, wouldn't you say?"

"I've talked to him about that," Casey said.

"They threatened to charge me with possession of stolen merchandise, and they bullied me in other ways too, but I didn't know anything. I just told them a man by the name of Simon gave it to me. They told me it was you."

"Obviously, they didn't charge you," Casey said.

"They wanted to know all about you, but I told them I didn't discuss my love life with strangers."

"They didn't have a chance in the world of getting a prosecutor to take a case like that. I knew that and I wouldn't have put you in that situation. I thought there was no way in the world that would have come back on you. I didn't think anyone would ever see that helmet out here," Casey said, revealing a tinge of guilt.

"I checked the internet to find out about the ISGM robbery. It was a short jump to realize that you did it."

Casey didn't say anything. He rolled over onto his side to get a better look at her expression. "I did it," he said.

Savanah was still staring at the ceiling. "I checked you out on Google. You're a lawyer from Springfield, Illinois. Are you still practicing?"

"Not really. I work pro bono mostly. I try to help people who can't afford legal counsel."

The robbery was still on Savanah's mind, but she was curious about Casey's personal life. That was a good sign to Casey. She had never questioned anything. It was all about the here and now, nothing about the future or the past. It felt good that she was interested in his life.

"How do you live if you work for free?"

It's a long story, but I'll make it brief. I represented an indigent junk yard owner back in 1990 for buzzing the Illinois State Capitol in a helicopter. It turned out that he wasn't so indigent. He left me the junk yard, and the copter. I sold the junk cars, trucks and parts for two hundred thousand."

"Two hundred thousand doesn't sound like enough to live the rest of your life."

"He left me a bundle of Microsoft stock too."

"Oh, yes, that would do it," Savanah said.

"Did he help you rob the museum?"

Casey chuckled, "No, his only crime was failing to report his net worth to the court and getting free counsel at the State's expense."

"Why did you do it – the robbery? You're a lawyer, and you have money?"

Casey thought about the question. It was actually two questions. Why are you so dissatisfied with life that you would take the chance, and why isn't being a lawyer enough?

He didn't answer immediately. He thought about it, but he already knew the answer to both. "I hate lawyers. They're greedy, but the greed isn't why I despise them. The worst part is they will ruin anyone's life just to win a case. I'm not made like that. I don't get any satisfaction from it." he said.

"Okay, but why did you rob the museum?"

"I don't know why I do anything, Savanah. I'll use the excuse that I did it because the owner is a pretentious, self-important, elitist, but that's just an excuse. The truth is I don't know why I did it. I don't know why I do anything."

"Why did you come back here?"

"That one is much easier. The two weeks I spent here with you were the most meaningful days of my life. I've thought about you nearly every day since I left here with that scarecrow in my rearview mirror. I feel like you and I are both cut from the same cloth, but there isn't a word for it. I can't explain it because it's inexplainable. I just feel it. That's all."

"Wow, I'm glad that was easy," Savanah said, displaying her vague little smile. Casey laughed.

Casey stayed with Savanah for eleven days before heading back to Illinois. When he left, she said, "I'll see you when you come back." It was different from the last time she said goodbye.

Chapter Fifteen

Agents Ford and Green met with the US Attorney, District of Massachusetts, Lyle Hammond on Monday morning after their conversation with Casey Rakestraw. When they entered, Hammond was friendly. He knew both Agents from a previous case he had handled on infamous mob member Robert Swag. They were assigned a frivolous case on possession of illegal native American artifacts as a means of punishing Lee Ford because the bureau chief had a grudge against him, but things ballooned, and Ford and Green brought down an entire mob family in New Jersey and Manhattan. Hammond believed Ford handled the case masterfully, so he campaigned for Ford to get the stalled ISGM case. It was twenty-four years old when the case landed in Ford's lap. Green was still a rookie under Ford's supervision, but they were tight.

Hammond stood up and walked around his desk to greet Ford and Green. "I've been looking at your reports. It's a sure thing you're on the right track," he said.

"We thought maybe it's time to bring him in," Ford said.

"Really? We don't have the stolen goods."

"No, nothing but the Roman Galea," Ford said.

"That was strange, don't you think? That scarecrow thing - What the hell!"

"He's a strange guy. He's smart. He never steps on

his own dick, but I think he's slipping, or maybe he's tired of all the drama."

"How's that?" Hammond asked.

"He gave up information about Evie Rainforth. He knew all about her situation. Nobody but the guy in that sketch would have known that."

"You mean the girl who thought he was a Martian?"

"Same one, but nobody knew about her except him, and he would have had to have been there."

"Maybe we can put things in chronological order," Hammond said, opening a manila folder with a printout of the reports. "March 15th, 1990, the heist goes down. The perps disappear without a trace. Evie Rainforth describes the man with the flying machine, a UFO, or what we think was a helicopter that came down in the grass at the amphitheater. From her description a police sketch was made of a man who looks like Casey Rakestraw. The next thing in order is that we have Rakestraw closing a deal for a client on a piece of land in Maple Creek, Oklahoma, in 1995. We didn't get the information on the galea until 1999 when it turned up on a scarecrows head in Maple Creek in Savanah Anderson's garden, and from information we got from the rural mail carrier it had been there since 1995," Ford said.

That means he was there, and no doubt he put that helmet on the scarecrow," Green said.

Hammond chuckled, "That was weird, wasn't it? I mean, hell's fire! A three-hundred-thousand-dollar collector's item stuck on a scarecrow's head!" Ford and Green both smiled. "It is," Ford agreed.

"The fact that Brenner, a friend from his time in the Army just happened to be a former security guard at

ISGM, and an old buddy from Vietnam taught him how to fly a copter. That's circumstantial evidence, but solid." Hammond said.

"He represented Jason Keys when Keys roughed up Dean Allen Marlow, that's another brick in the wall," Green said.

"That's a good case if I ever saw one. Why did it take so long to get here?" Hammond said.

"It all came in piece by piece, Lyle. Nobody was laying down on the job," Ford said.

"Oh, I know that, but I'm just saying it's a slam dunk."

"Then we make an arrest?" Ford asked.

Hammond rubbed his chin. "We don't have physical evidence. Have we questioned Keys and Brenner?"

"No, but they've both been under surveillance for a long time. We're monitoring their cell phones. They are being very careful about communication because we haven't heard a thing that would help us."

"Let's interrogate them before we make an arrest. Maybe one of them, or both will turn belly up," Hammond said. The conversation ended on that note.

On Tuesday morning, Ford and Green were flown from Boston to Peoria, Illinois via, bureau jet. They rented a car and drove to Kewanee and located Louie's Antique Store on South Main Street. When they walked into the store, Brenner, a pale complexioned man with gray hair standing behind a small counter, leaning over examining paperwork on the countertop.

"Is Louie here," Ford asked.

"Louie's dead," he said, looking up, placing his elbows on the counter.

"How about Jake Brenner?" Ford said, displaying

his shield.

The man didn't have to answer. Fear was immediately visible in his eyes. His hands started shaking like a feather under a ceiling fan. "I'm Jake Brenner, why," he said, his voice cracking.

"We need to talk, Mr. Brenner," Ford said.

"Why, why would the FBI want to talk to me?"

Green stepped around to the end of the counter. He knew by closing the gap between them Brenner would feel trapped. "We need to ask you some questions," he said.

"How long will it take? Will I need to close the store?"

"Probably," Green said.

Brenner's expression was as good as a confession. Pleading and fear were plastered all over his face and in his glaring eyes. He dug into the drawer beneath the countertop and pulled out a key ring. The keys were jingling like a wind chime as Brenner continued shaking. The world was about to turn sideways and flip through the universe.

After locking the door and flipping the closed sign, Brenner stood with his back against the door biting his fingernails. "If I go to jail, they'll rape me and kill me," he whispered aloud.

"What was that you said?" Green asked.

"Nothing. I, ahh, it was nothing," Brenner mumbled.

They walked through the cluttered store to a small office in the back. Brenner pulled up chairs for Ford and Green and then sat on the desk. Ford raised his palm with fingers spread, "No, get another chair and sit down," Ford said. Brenner was obedient. Ford slid his chair close to Brenner's chair and leaned forward.

Brenner's eyes were the size of saucers. Ford stared at Brenner without speaking. Suddenly it was like basic training when Sergeant Lloyd Lilly got up in Brenner's face. When Brenner looked into Agent Ford's eyes, he snorted and giggled covering his mouth, spit spewing into the air. Ford and Green looked at each other - astonished.

When Brenner had regained control of himself, Ford asked him directly if he had robbed the ISG Museum. It was against every rule in the book, but Ford thought Brenner would break immediately. He wasn't wrong, but it didn't go the way he expected.

"Can we make a deal?" Brenner asked.

"The Supreme Court says that we can't make deals. Tit for tat, you know, quid pro quo. Everything you tell us under those conditions is inadmissible."

"I've heard that people make deals," Brenner said.

"I've heard that too," Ford said.

"How do they do that?"

"The District Attorney can ask for immunity, but all we can tell you is that you will feel better if you get this off your chest," Ford said.

"I'm not talking until I get immunity, and an attorney,"

"Suit yourself," Ford said, scooting his chair out to get up. Green said, "You're making a mistake Jake. You'll feel a lot better if you get this off your chest."

When the agents were back in their car Green said, "If we would have had a chance to question him, he'd be spilling his guts right now."

"I wanted to lead him into it, but he went straight to wanting a deal, and an attorney. That screwed it up right from the start. I shouldn't have asked him straight out," Ford said. They were quiet for a moment. Green chuckled. "Have you ever seen a reaction like that?

"You mean snorting and giggling?"

"Yeah, what the hell!" Green laughed.

"It was weird." Ford said.

Chapter Sixteen

When Casey got back to Illinois, he stopped at Mickey's for a beer. The place was dark and empty, just the way he liked it. He took a seat at the end of the bar where he could see the tv. Judge Judy was giving the plaintiff hell as usual. Helen, the bartender brought Casey a Blue Moon without asking. When she sat it down, she said, "Jason Keys was here yesterday. He said if I see you, you need to get in contact."

Casey didn't ask her why. If Jason needed to talk it was serious.

Casey placed a five on the counter and headed for the door. Helen picked up the bottle and took a drink. She toasted Casey as he walked out.

As Casey was approaching Virden on route 4, oncoming cars were flashing their head lights. Jason was sitting at the empty gas station lot with a handheld radar gun. Casey pulled in beside him and rolled down his window. "What's up Jason?"

Jason laid the radar gun down in the seat. "I had a little surprise visit yesterday," he said.

"I'm listening," Casey said.

"FBI agents came to city hall asking for me. The dispatcher called me in, and when I got there, they were sitting in my office."

"Agents Ford and Green?"

"No, it was Frederick and Shay."

"Tell me about it."

"They wanted to ask me about the heist. I politely

told them I didn't have time to talk. One of them, I can't remember which, ask me if I wanted to take the fifth. I told them I wasn't taking the fifth, I just wasn't going to answer their questions.

"How'd they take that?"

"Oh, they tried to bully me, but I just asked them politely to leave."

"And they left?"

"Yeah, they left, but they were jawing at me the whole way. They talked like they were gonna take me in and put me under oath. I just said, okay, I'll see you then."

"I wonder if they know about Billy. Did they talk to Billy?"

"No, I had a beer with Billy at Mickey's. I asked him if he had visitors. He knew what I was talking about, but he kept zipping his fingers across his lips every time I asked a question. It was comical. If they ever get him in, they're gonna think he's retarded."

Casey laughed, "That's not all bad, is it?"

After that they sat in silence for a long time. Finally, Jason said, "You know, Casey, I loved being a cop, it was my whole life. I never thought I'd be a thief or do anything outside the law. Even now in this little berg I try to do a good job. I know the law, and I practice in my mind how to talk to people in order to be a servant to the public. I still feel like a cop. I'm not ashamed of what we did. Am I a hypocrite?"

"If some money comes our way from this, and we take it, we're both hypocrites, but I think that presumption would be mitigated by the fact Marlo is the real criminal. In a fight you have a right to strike back. Marlo drew first blood. You had a right to defend yourself, and I'm in this fight too. I'm not ashamed, but I don't like to lie, and lying is the only regret I have. My skin crawls when I lie, but I'm gonna do it anyway. I'm not going to jail if I can help it. That would be like a twelve round boxing match and losing in a split decision. I want to beat Marlo in this game."

"What should I do if they take me in and put me under oath"

"Take the fifth, they don't have anything on you. Talking to them would be the only way you can hurt yourself.

"Catch you later," Casey said, rolling up his car window as he drove away.

He drove back into town and went to Springfield Capitol Airport. He purchased a one-way ticket to Logan International in Boston. It would be three days wait before his flight, and the thought had crossed his mind that the FBI might pick him up at any given moment. It was time to pull the ace out of his sleeve, but he would have to be free to get it done. If he was behind bars the jig was up. Later he would alter his plans and the ticket for the flight would go unused. He was at a point where he could change his plans at a given moment.

Agents Ford and Green had been in contact with US Attorney Hammond regarding Brenner's demand for immunity and an attorney. Hammond gave the go ahead to get Brenner in to get a statement. The Agents had stayed in Kewanee at the Motel 6. It wasn't what they were accustomed to, but they had lodged in worse. After they got the word from Hammond, they drove the short distance to Louie's Antique Store. When they walked in Brenner looked just as panicked as he had the first time.

"Put your closed sign up." Green said as he approached the counter.

"Why!"

"You're taking a little trip to Massachusetts."

"I can't go to Massachusetts!"

"You can either go voluntarily, or we can put you under arrest," Ford said

"Do I get immunity?"

"The case regarding the ISG Museum will go to court in Massachusetts. The US Attorney is offering you immunity, and the State prosecutor is offering a letter of immunity. That means you're good to go. US Attorney Hammond who will represent the government wants to have you in his office to sign the agreement and get your confession."

"Confession! What do you mean?"

"You're immunity in exchange for your admission for your participation in the robbery. That's a confession, Mr. Brenner."

Brenner thought about it for a moment. "Okay, I need to get a bag, I guess. We can't get to Boston and back today, can we?"

"You got that right, Jake. Get busy," Green said.

Two hours later they were in the bureau jet headed to the east coast.

Chapter Seventeen

In Nineteen sixty-four, Casey Rakestraw was a senior in high school. Cancer took his mother when he was fifteen years old. He and his father, Robert Rakestraw were living in a beat-up mobile home on the blacktop road south of Delavan, Illinois. Robert was an energetic guy who could do anything he set his mind to, but if he had two nickels to rub together having a job wasn't a necessity. Sometimes he was full of gospel and at other times he preached against religion as being the cause of every ill on earth. Robert liked his beer and loved the Delavan Tap.

Casey worked in the local pool hall cleaning tables and racking tables for lunch money. It wasn't easy being a high school senior under those conditions. Casey never forgot about how it was in those days, and that was the reason he was sympathetic to people down on their luck. Representing them pro bono was his way of paying it forward.

Everything that had happened was weighing on Casey's mind as he was waiting at the employee entrance to the courthouse when Billy came out of the building. Billy's shirt was untucked, his tie was three inches too short, and his pants a size too big. Casey honked the horn to get his attention. When Billy saw him, his face lit up.

"Get in," Casey said.

"What's up?" Billy asked.

"I'm going to Boston for a few days, I thought we

could get a beer and hang out for a while. Have you got plans?"

"I was gonna pick up a pizza and watch Dances With Wolves again," Billy said.

"So, you're busy?"

"Noo!. Let's go," Billy said, pulling his tie loose and pitching it into the back seat.

Casey stopped at the liquor store on Grand Avenue and bought a twelve pack of Blue Moon, and a six pack of Coke. He drove north out of town. "We're taking a little road trip," he said. He popped the first Blue Moon and handed Billy a Coke. Billy shook his head and pointed to the box with the beer in it. They took I-55 to Williamsville and cut over to the Peoria blacktop. When they reached their destination the first two beers were gone. Casey stopped in the middle of the road and pointed to an old trailer sitting between two trees, overrun with weeds, caving in on one end, and rusted through near the opening where the door used to be. "There's my humble abode," he said.

"You own it?" Billy asked.

"Yep, it's all mine."

"Nice," Billy said.

Billy stared out the window with a blank look on his face. "Your curiosity is amazing," Casey said.

"Why?" Billy asked, turning to look at Casey. That childlike expression prominent in his eyes. "That's where my Pop and I lived for four years."

"Nice," Billy said again.

"You wouldn't think by looking at that, that I would be sitting on top of five hundred million dollars' worth of illicit goods, would you?"

Billy glared at Casey with raised eyebrows. He took

his finger and thumb and zipped them across his lips. Casey laughed. Billy took his fingers again and reversed the zipping motion. "Is that where they are?" He asked. His high-pitched voice an octave higher than before. He re-zipped his lips in slow motion.

"No, and I wouldn't tell you if I could. It would just put you in greater jeopardy," Casey said.

Billy didn't seem interested in the history of the trailer at all. "Nothing to see here, I guess," Casey said, putting the car into gear. They left and drove north to route 122, turned and headed east. Billy reached across the seat and grabbed two more beers. They crossed the interstate and pulled into the parking lot of the Hopedale Auction Barn. Weeds and saplings were growing around the barn and grass and twigs were visible in the rain gutters. The roof was rotting in places where shingles had blown away. They sat quietly for a few moments while Brown Eyed Girl played on the radio.

"I used to scoop shit in there, Billy," Casey said.

"It's out of business," Billy said.

"You're right about that, Mr. Obvious," Casey said, taking a drink from his can. Billy took a drink too.

Their next stop was on the Dillon blacktop, north of Delavan at the Mackinaw River bridge. There was a mud road leading from the blacktop to a bare spot beneath the bridge where evidence of numerous campfires and beer parties had left it a total mess. Casey drove to the river's edge, parked and turned up his beer and downed it. Billy rolled down his window and pitched his empty can out onto the ground.

"Go get it," Casey said.

Billy looked bewildered. "There's cans

everywhere," he said.

"We didn't bring'em." Casey said. Billy reluctantly got out of the car and retrieved his can. Casey handed him a plastic bag to put it in.

"My dad brought me down here when I was a senior in high school. We drank twelve beers, and I was drunk before we left. Pop was drunk so he made me drive. The lines were crisscrossing on the road, and I had my face plastered to the windshield. I said, "Pop I'm too drunk to drive. He said, you'll be alright, Casey, just keep it between the ditches."

"Did you get arrested?"

"Nope, but he did."

"For lettin' you drive drunk?"

"No, armed robbery. The cops pulled us over in Tremont right after we drove into town. Cars and cops came from everywhere with guns pointed at us, yelling like that stuff you see on tv. They pulled Pop out of the car and slammed him face first onto the ground and handcuffed him."

"What happened after that? Why didn't they arrest you?"

"I don't know, Billy, I was sure drunk, but they weren't interested in me. They took me to a truck stop and left me there. They told me to call someone to come and get me. I didn't have anyone to call, so I walked thirteen miles home."

"What happened to your dad?"

"He went to prison. The last time I saw him was when I visited him in the Tazewell County Jail. I asked him why he did it. He said, I don't know Casey. I don't know why I do anything."

Billy held his drink up and leaned over towards

Casey. Casey clicked his can in a toast. Clicking their drinks together. An act that was an affirmation of support or agreement between them.

Chapter Eighteen

While enroute to Boston, Brenner tried to get answers from Ford and Green, but when Green said, "Jake, anything you say can and will be used against you in a court of law," Brenner said. "I thought I was getting immunity,"

"We told you we can't make promises. If you make statements to us before you get your deal from the US Attorney, and the District Attorney, we'll have to testify to that in court," Green said.

"If you want to waive your rights, we're ready to have a go at it," Ford said.

"Ah, I don't think so," Brenner said.

It was quiet for the rest of the flight. Ford and Green paged through printouts and Brenner sat looking straight ahead. When they reached Boston International, there was a car waiting for them. It was a quick trip downtown. Hammond was waiting in his office with a video camera set up and a court shorthand reporter on hand. The District Attorney's Letter of Immunity was on Hammond's desk, and a Statutory Order was signed by District Judge Arthur Garcia. After Hammond introduced himself, he explained each document in detail. Brenner was like a deer caught in the headlights but still had presence of mind to ask about the Statutory Order. Although Brenner's statement would be voluntary, the order was binding, holding Brenner to mandatorily testifying in court, but also granting him total immunity from prosecution. It was a good deal, but it still made him nervous.

Hammond started by stating his name, the time, the names of the others who were present, and then asked Brenner to state his name and his age. The sound of the court reporter's keys were clicking, and the red light on the video recorder blinking. Brenner leaned over to the microphone and started to say his name but when he opened his mouth, he made a grunting sound and then broke out in a giggling fit. His eyes were bulging as he looked at Hammond, and tears were running down his cheek.

Hammond called for a break. He pulled Ford aside and asked if he thought Brenner might do that in court. Ford shrugged, "I don't know, Lyle, he might,"

"That's not good!"

They restarted the process, and Brenner had stopped giggling. "Tell us in your own words about the Ida Swigert Graham Museum robbery, and how you were involved," Hammond said. "Do you know Casey Rakestraw?" He added.

"Yes, I do."

"Tell us about Casey Rakestraw and your association with him."

"I met Casey when we were in basic training in 1966."

"Did you ever see him operating a helicopter?"

"No, but I heard he was a good friend of a really well-known Huey pilot when we were in Vietnam."

"Did his friend teach him how to operate a helicopter?"

"That was the rumor."

"Can you tell us about your association with him and what you know about the ISG Museum theft?"

"Well, when we were transferring out of Vietnam, I saw him in a bar. We talked about what we had done before we were drafted. I told him all about a job I had as a security guard at the ISG Museum. It was really a laxed place for having so many valuable things – world famous stuff. Casey laughed about it. He thought it was bad that they depended on somebody like me to keep the place safe. I never thought about it again until he came to see me where I live in Kewanee, Illinois, in 1990. He said he wanted to rob the place and asked if I wanted in on it."

"You had never considered robbing the museum before he made the proposal?"

"Well, I did think about how easy it would be, but I never really thought about doing it myself. Not until Casey ask me to help."

"What did you do? I mean by that what was your participation?"

"Casey paid for our trip to Boston where we stayed for a few days, or maybe a week. It was a long time ago; I don't remember exactly how many days we were there."

"Tell us what you did."

"We visited the museum, and I showed Casey where the alarm button was behind the security desk. Well, we didn't really see behind the desk, but I told him where it was. There were security cameras too, and they were all out in the open. I showed him where all the valuable paintings were hung and stuff like that. We walked through it several times, and I made notes for him about when and where we made our rounds. It was simple. Nothing had changed since I was there. It was all the same."

"According to our reports, two men dressed like policemen approached the employee entrance and ordered the guards to let them in. Isn't that against policy? Wouldn't that be a policy violation to let them in?"

"Yes, it was a violation, but I'd probably done the same thing. The only training we got was sort of an introduction to the job, and a handbook we were supposed to study."

"Were you, or Casey one of those men dressed in police uniforms?"

"No, I wasn't, and I don't think Casey was either, but I can't swear to it. Casey never gave me the names of the others involved. I asked him once after the robbery how it went down, but he wouldn't tell me. He said the less I knew about it the better it would be if I ever got questioned by the police."

"Can you tell me where the paintings are now?"

"No, I don't know where they are, but I know Casey has them."

"Did you receive money from them?"

"No, Casey tried to find someone to launder them for us, but he didn't find anyone. I called him a lot of times, but his answer was always the same. I even accused him of selling them and cutting me out, but that wasn't true, and I knew it. I was just trying to get him to work harder on selling that stuff. I needed money."

"You used a pay phone, I'm guessing."

"Yes, always a pay phone. Casey told me never to use my home phone or a cell phone."

"Did you go to Charleston with Casey to meet Marcel Corelli to try to get him involved in selling the paintings?"

"No, I went alone, and I didn't know the guy's name. I found his number in Louie's notes, the guy who used to own my antique store. They had some kind of thing going on about a picture that was supposed to be stolen from the Jews during World War Two. Anyway, I just heard them talking and I put two and two together. I called the number and set up a meeting. I was already in Charleston when I called Casey to fill him in. He got mad about it. He thought I was being set up, so he drove all night from Illinois to come out there to take over. The deal didn't go down and the guy was arrested a few days later. That really scared Casey and he said we need to lay low. I tried to call him several times over the years, but he wouldn't pick up my calls. I got the point that we were never getting rid of that stuff."

Hammond wasn't convinced that Brenner didn't know where the valuables were and threatened him with nullifying the agreement and prosecuting him for perjury if he learned that Brenner had lied in any manner during their interview. They went over Brenner's testimony several times in detail before he was released. Brenner was flown back to Peoria, Illinois and ordered not to leave the state without permission from the US Attorney's office.

Chapter Nineteen

After Casey's road trip with Billy, he drove to Lake Wasabi, to his cabin office. He had his Sawzall with him, a tool he hadn't used since the day he cut the vent pipe in 1995. That was a long time between uses. He went inside and in just moments he was through. He was never worried about the paintings being damaged inside the pipe. It was never hooked to the sewage line, and it was airtight. It was secured on the concrete floor, anchored to a t-stand he had installed to make it look more authentic. When he pulled the pipe away from the connector the paintings slid out one by one. He packed them in an army duffle bag and put them into the trunk of his car. If the FBI had an arrest warrant out for him and they stopped him, he would be headed straight to prison. There was no way to explain how he happened to have five hundred million dollars' worth of stolen merchandise in the trunk of his car. A warrant for his arrest was almost a guarantee, as far as he was concerned. If he had a client in his position, he would already be vying for a lenient sentence. He knew the Feds had a good case against him and it wouldn't be long before they came calling. Now it was a race against time.

Casey had a credit card from Gabby's Auto Salvage he kept active throughout the years. It came in handy when he was trying to stay covert. He purchased three gift cards from Walmart and bought three burner phones with them before going to the airport. If the

Feds knew about the phones it was possible for them to follow the pings when they were used but they first had to know about them. It wasn't likely they would be able to trace them back to Casey.

Casey drove to General Mitchell International Airport in Milwaukee, Wisconsin. He bought a one-way ticket to Boston International. Upon his arrival, he rented a car from Hertz, drove to the Holiday Inn, and checked in. He used the first burner to call a number listed on a site posted by the ISG Museum administration offering a reward of twelve million dollars for the return of the paintings. It was a recording directing calls regarding the painting to the Leon Brady Law Firm.

Casey called the number listed for the attorney, a man answered, "Leon Brady." Casey wasn't surprised. When you were talking about something as serious as the heist and a twelve-million-dollar reward, a dedicated line made sense.

"I'm calling about the ISGM robbery," Casey said.

"Yes, of course you are, this line is designated for that purpose. Do you have information?

"I'm an attorney. I represent a client who can guarantee the return of the items taken in the robbery."

"Go ahead, I'm listening," Brady said. His tone seemed like he was as interested as a man choosing toppings for a pizza.

"You probably get calls like this all the time, I'm guessing."

"You're right about that."

"This is the real deal, Mr. Brady."

"Do you have proof?"

"I've got polaroid pictures of the paintings."

"That's not really proof. It would be an easy process to take pictures from a magazine with a polaroid."

"It's not well-known what paintings were taken. I can tell you what they were, and I have a picture of each. Nobody would know about the Roman galea being left on a scarecrows head, but my client informed me that it was, and it was recovered in Oklahoma. That was information exclusive to the FBI and federal prosecutors."

"Really," Brady said. His tone of voice had changed. "What's the name of your firm, and your name?"

"We're not going there," Casey said.

"I don't know how we can do business without knowing who you are, and who you're representing."

"I need for you to contact Dean Allen Marlo and tell him that my client has the paintings and I have seen them. Tell him that he can have them back for the twelve million dollars his ad promised. Twelve million for 500 million is a good deal for him. Tell him that I'll provide a contract for him to sign guaranteeing that there will be no arrest or prosecution of the persons involved in the robbery. We can work out the details of the exchange after you have contacted him and relayed my demands. If the FBI makes an arrest regarding the robbery the paintings will be destroyed. If I learn that Marlo, his staff, or anyone of his legal team contacts the FBI all paintings will be burned.

"I'm assuming your client is guilty of robbing the museum and has possession of the items removed in the robbery. Is that right?"

"We're not discussing who, what, when or where until you get the word from Marlo," Casey said. He hit the end button and the phone went silent.

Agents Ford and Green were in Springfield, Illinois. They were waiting for the word from Lyle Hammond that an arrest warrant had been issued. The local FBI office had been notified to expect an arrest, and to be prepared. Now they were killing time.

"It's reasonable to believe Jason Keys was an accomplice in this case, but there has to be another person involved," Green said

"For sure," Ford said.

Green had a folder opened, paging through printouts. "We've checked out every client Rakestraw had for a five-year period prior to 1990. There's one guy here who seems to have gotten special treatment. Rakestraw represented him pro bono, and according to interviews Agents Frederick and Shay had done, Rakestraw took him under his wing. He got his record expunged and pulled strings to get him a job at the courthouse."

"Fredrick and Shay didn't interview the guy?"

"Nope."

"What's his name?"

"William Wiley."

After a short discussion They were headed for the courthouse. As they talked on the way, Ford said, "You know, I kind of like Rakestraw."

"Why?

"He was calm about everything, a little funny at times, and he knows we're closing in on him. He's a lawyer, but he looks like a salty old backwoodsman. He represents people free of charge, and helps people who are down on their luck"

"Well, he wasn't making fun of your ethnicity."

"That's because all Caucasians stick together, Ty."

"More truth to that than you think, Lee."

There was a picture of Billy in the file, so the agents waited outside the employee entrance at the courthouse. When Billy came out, he was wearing a yellow short-sleeve shirt, a blue tie that hung three inches above his waistline, and brown corduroy pants. His gray hair covered his ears.

When they spotted him Green said, "No way this guy was involved in a heist like the ISG Museum job."

"Stranger things, Ty, stranger things," Ford said.

When they got out of the car Billy stopped and watched them. They met him halfway up the sidewalk, each of them holding their badges. "FBI, Mr. Wiley, we need to talk."

"Why, Mr. FBI's. Why do we need to talk?"

"Just a few questions, Mr. Wiley."

"My friends call me, Billy."

"We can talk in the car, Billy, "Ford said.

When they were in the car, Billy was looking uneasy in the back seat. "Billy, do you know Casey Rakestraw?"

"Yeah, he's my friend."

Ford was watching Billy in the rearview mirror. Billy's eyes were shut, and his lips tight across his teeth. "How long have you known him?"

"A long time."

"Did you know him in 1990?"

Billy leaned his head against the back seat headrest and closed his eyes. Ford was watching him in the rearview mirror as he pressed his forefinger and thumb on his lips and zipped them shut. Ford turned in the seat to watch him. Green looked at Ford with a slight smile. Billy's eyes were closed as tight as a coffee can lid, and his jaws clinched.

"Are you alright, Billy?"

Billy unzipped his lips. "Yes," he said, and then rezipped them.

Ford chuckled. "What are you doing?"

"Am I under arrest," Billy asked without unzipping his lips. When he realized the answer had escaped without unzipping, he shook his head, grimaced and unzipped them and asked, "Am I under arrest?"

Ford and Green looked amused. "No, you're not under arrest, but your behavior is a little bizarre."

Billy zipped his lips and opened the car door to get out. "Stop, Billy, we need to ask you some questions," Ford said. Billy got out and walked away. Ford and Green both chuckled as the strange little man disappeared around the corner. "I guess he's not talking," Green said.

"He's all zipped up," Ford said. They both laughed again.

"He knows something, that's for sure, but my God, this is crazy. We've got a guy who giggles and snorts like a calf, and now a troll like guy who zips his lips. Rakestraw must be a genius or the luckiest crook on earth. Wow, I mean, we're talking about more money than we could count in a lifetime being on the line, and this is what we're dealing with," Ford said. They looked at each other in astonishment.

"We know Rakestraw did the robbery, but we're a long way from knowing everything we need to know before taking this case to court," Ford said. Ford put the car into drive and pulled away.

Chapter Twenty

Casey was sitting on the bed in his room when the burner rang. He waited for four rings before he hit the accept button. "Mr. Brady, is that you?" He asked.

"Yes, I've been in contact with Mr. Marlo. He wants to meet you to examine the polaroid pictures. He's bringing an art examiner with him."

"No," Casey said.

"Sir, we must have the polaroid pictures examined, or we can't move forward."

"I'll accept an art examiner having a look at the pictures, but no personal contact. I'll need to know the name of the examiner, his credentials, and a mailing address. Once that's been accomplished, call the number I gave you, and you'll receive further instructions."

Dean Allen Marlo, Leon Brady and Lyle Hammond were sitting in Hammonds office during the conversation between Brady and Casey. Hammond expression was dour, his brow furrowed, and jaws pinioned. It was apparent he didn't like the situation. "We need to get my agents in here to get a location on that cell phone," he said.

"Absolutely not," Marlo said.

Hammond's expression changed only by his eyes shifting from Marlo to Brady. "I'm going to prosecute this case. We have at least one suspect we're ready to bring in right now. I want these guys, Leon, and I'm gonna get them!"

Leon Brady rubbed his chin, uncrossed his legs and placed both feet on the floor. He leaned forward. "Lyle, we came to you because we didn't want a surprise arrest coming down while we're negotiating. If an arrest is made before we get those paintings, five hundred million is going up in smoke."

"That is utter bullshit, my friend!" Hammond said.

"It may be, but that's the deal. We'll give you everything once we have that art back in our hands," Marlo said, getting up, straightening his jacket. "One other thing. I'm attending a luncheon with Senator Bertrand this afternoon; the Attorney General will probably be there. Do I need to bring this up to him?"

Hammond glared at Marlo, waited for a long moment and said, "No."

Marlo and Brady left the office and called for Marlo's car. As they drove back to the Brady law office, they made a call to Casey. They were ready with the information Casey wanted, including a post office box where the pictures could be mailed. When Casey got the information, he slipped on surgical gloves, washed the pictures thoroughly with soap and water, placed them in a plastic bag and walked four blocks to an independent mailing service. He used an envelope provided by the clerk, addressed it and dropped it into the box. He was careful never to contact the envelope with his skin. Casey believed he would get the money Marlo had offered, but he also knew they would be trying to nail him even after the exchange. Getting DNA off those pictures would be a routine matter for the FBI.

Billy Wiley didn't know how to get ahold of Casey. He knew he was in Boston, but he didn't know why.

Billy was concerned because he had been approached by the FBI, and Billy didn't become concerned easily. He stopped at Mickey's and left word with Helen that he needed to talk to Casey or Jason if they came in. "I'll tie a string on my finger, Billy," she said. Billy gave her the thumbs up sign and headed home.

Jake Brenner was back in Kewanee, Illinois, pacing aimlessly through the cluttered Iles in his junk store. He had given US Attorney Hammond everything he knew about the heist, and about Casey Rakestraw. He was safe from prosecution, but it was his nature to worry, and fret about everything. Somehow this was going to blow back on him, and he knew it. The more he thought about it, the more convinced he was that he had to act. Several times he picked up his cell phone and keyed up Casey's number, only to put it back down without calling. Finally with shaking hands he picked up the phone and hit the send button.

Casey was sitting on his bed, both feet on the floor, his hands dangling between his knees when the phone rang. When he saw Brenner's number he sighed, "Shit," and then, "Hello."

"Casey, it's me," he said.

"Yeah, Jake, what's up?"

"I told them, Casey," he said, releasing a faint snort, and a blubbering sound.

Casey was quiet for a long moment. "What did you tell, and who did you tell it to?" He already knew the answer to his question. Shaky Jake Brenner didn't have the spine of an earth worm. Casey's biggest worry for the last twenty-five years had been that Jake would be questioned by the FBI.

"I told the FBI and the US Attorney." Jake snorted

again.

"Why, Jake. You were never going to be prosecuted, even if they arrested me. You guys were all safe."

"I was scared, Casey. They gave me immunity. I'm sorry."

"Blanket immunity?" Casey asked

"Transitional Immunity. That's what they call it. It was signed by a judge. If it goes to court, I'll have to testify."

"That's blanket immunity. Did you tell them others were involved?"

"I did, but I didn't know the names of the other guys. You wouldn't tell me. And that's probably good, right?"

Casey clinched his jaw and tightened his lips. At that moment he wanted to choke Brenner. Since he couldn't do that, he decided to put a scare into him. "You don't know them, Jake, but they know you. Let that sink in."

"Casey, please, I'm sorry."

"Since you called me from your cell, they're probably listening, and tracking my phone. Don't call me again, Jake." He hung up, walked to the duffle bag on the floor, picked it up and walked out the door. As he left the hotel, he dropped his cell phone into the trash can at the exit.

Fifteen minutes later four FBI agents showed up. They were looking for Casey. His room was searched but it was empty. Every waste basket on each floor was searched before they found Casey's cell in the trash can at the exit. At that moment Casey became a man on the run.

Lee Ford and Tyrese Green were circling the block in downtown Springfield. They were stopped at the traffic light at Adams and 6th Street. The sun was just sinking below the roofline of the historic Herndon, Lincoln Law Office. Ford was reciting everything he knew about Abraham Lincoln when his cell phone rang. It was Lyle Hammond. "We need to pick up Rakestraw if we can locate him. I think he's making a deal with Marlo for the reward money."

Ford didn't answer immediately. "Humph, he's a smart sonofabitch," he said.

"What do you mean by that?"

"It's the only way he can get out of this. He makes a deal with Marlo, takes the reward and disappears. Ah, and I guess there's no arrest warrant."

"No, I've talked to Marlo and his attorney, Leon Brady. They're in contact with someone who has the paintings, vying for a deal and I'm sure it's him."

"But they don't know it's him?"

"No, and I didn't tell them. They asked me – no they threatened me. They don't want an arrest until after the completion of the exchange. They don't want us anywhere near it."

"How can they threaten you – a US Attorney?"

"Marlo has a US Senator in his pocket, and he rubs elbows with the Attorney General."

"Swamp rats?" Green interjected.

"Yep."

"So, we need to bring him in? Won't that go against what they asked?"

"They don't know what we know. They don't know it's Rakestraw they're talking to. It's just an unknown intermediary to them."

"I'm guessing they don't want us involved because they think they'll lose the paintings if we take him down."

"Exactly."

"Can we monitor the situation, and then move in once the exchange has been made?"

"No, they won't cooperate. Brady said they would give us everything they have after the paintings are recovered, but nothing until then. That's why we need to get Rakestraw in. When the FBI takes him in for questioning, they'll have to come to me to stop the Bureau from throwing a monkey wrench into the deal. That's when I lay down some restrictions." Hammond said.

"So, we're wasting time here in Springfield?"

"Yes, for now. The local office here in Boston got a ping on Rakestraw's cell phone. It was at a Holiday Inn. When they got there Rakestraw was gone, and his cell was in the trash can at the exit."

"We're headed back to Washington. We'll call you when we get in," Ford said.

When Hammond disconnected, Ford looked at Green with a grimace. "These politicians and civilians are gonna fuck things up for us," he said.

Casey didn't know the capabilities of the FBI concerning tracking burner phones, but he assumed they could digitally locate the pings off local towers. It was a stretch to think they could find a burner purchased with a gift card in Wisconsin by pings in Boston, Massachusetts, but he knew they had his personal cell phone locked in. That was the difference. Homeland security could digitally monitor every call in North America; what they did with the information was anybody's guess, but he wasn't taking any chances. He needed to put some distance between himself and the Holiday Inn. It was better to be safe than sorry.

He was driving without a destination when he hit Morrissey boulevard, headed toward Carson Beach. There was one spot left in the parking lot near the water, so he pulled in and stopped. He sat there for several minutes looking across the beach as tourist moseyed along the pedestrian walkways, with coats pulled close against their ribs. Dreary looking clouds were on the horizon, and gray water lapped against the sand. Casey was wearing a flannel shirt beneath a tan Carhart coat. He looked a little out of place, but not so much as to draw attention. He had shaved his beard and mustache when he visited Savanah, but it was nearly back to its normal length.

The temperature in Boston wasn't like the biting cold of Wisconsin, but it was damp and frigid coming off Boston Harbor. Casey walked across Morrissey to a bench facing the beach. The boats in the harbor were veiled in moist air, barely visible in the distance. Casey rubbed his hands and blew on them to ward off the cold. His eyes were fixed on the horizon as he mulled over his situation. Brenner had sunk his plans to operate from the Holiday Inn, so he needed to find another place to stay. Now he was afraid to use his Gabby's Auto Salvage credit card. It was a cinch that the FBI had connected his room and cell phone to the card. He wasn't concerned he had been identified. Ford and Green had as much as said they were coming after him when they were in Wisconsin. Minutes and hours mattered more than anonymity.

Casey was still looking out to sea when he heard a voice singing, and boots stomping along the boardwalk. He saw a guy with a long-tattered coat, frayed gloves, and a stocking cap pulled tight over his ears. He stopped in front of Casey and glared at him from strange steel gray eyes. "Would you help a guy out?" He asked.

Casey didn't speak but reached into his front pocket and pulled out a ten-dollar bill. He handed it to the man without making eye contact. "Thanks partner," the guy said. Casey waited for him to move on, but he stood there with the money in his hand. "Mind if I sit for a while," he asked.

Casey shrugged, "No, go ahead, sit."

They were both quiet. It was hard for Casey to continue to think about his next move with a homeless man sitting next to him. They were both watching the ships in the harbor.

The guy started singing again, "Distant ships sailing into the mist, you were born with a snake in both of your fist while a hurricane was blowing."

"Humm, Bob Dylan?" Casey asked.

"Yep, Joker Man."

"America's poet," Casey said.

The guy hummed for a moment and then sang quietly, "Freedom just around the corner for you, but the truth so far off, what good will it do?"

Casey chuckled, "Are your reading my mind," he said.

"No. I'm just a messed-up guy who gets it."

"Do you live here on the beach?"

"No, I've got a place under the overpass on I-95 near the Red Line."

The guy was wearing rags, but he wasn't dirty. A rust-colored beard and hair were bristling as if he had been struck by lightning, but they were clean. There must have been something in Casey's stare that signaled what he was thinking so the man responded. "These restrooms along the beach all have showers in them. I shower almost every day," he said.

"Well," Casey said.

"When I came upon you, your expression revealed a man in serious contemplation, sir," he said.

Casey glanced at the guy sideways. "You don't sound like the homeless people I usually run into," he said.

"I'm an educated man, sir. Philosophy major."

"Really?"

"Yep, PhD, in fact."

The corners of Casey's lips turned up. A warm expression visible in his eyes as he looked into the distance. Yeah, he's a PhD and I'm Julius Caesar," Casey thought.

"Philosophy will drive you crazy" the man said. "How about you? What do you do besides stare at the ocean?"

"I'm a lawyer."

"You don't look like a lawyer."

"You don't look like a philosopher." Casey said, and then hesitated, "Well, maybe you do," he added. It was surreal sitting there amid all that was happening talking with a homeless man. And then reality seeped into his thoughts. Brady had plenty of time to call, but he hadn't. Something wrong, maybe?

"The greatest way to live with honor in this life is to be what we pretend to be," The guy said.

"Bob Dylan again?"

"No, Socrates."

"It's been nice talking to you," Casey said, getting up. He needed a place to stay and gather his thoughts. "Well, good luck, my friend," he said. Casey walked towards his car. As he waited for cars to pass on Morrissey Street a bizarre thought crossed his mind. The beach philosopher was still looking at him through those strange clear steel-colored eyes. There was an innocent curiosity in his expression. "I need a place to stay," Casey said. "Me casa, su casa, my friend," the philosopher said. His eyebrows raised as he shrugged his shoulders.

I must be crazy, but I'm thinking, yes. I've slept in a muddy bunker in Vietnam, how could this be worse? he thought. But then it occurred to him that he was twenty when he did that, and now he was seventy-four. He crossed the road to his car and retrieved the duffle bag containing his ill-gotten cargo.

"Lead the way." Casey said.

Chapter Twenty-One

As Casey walked with the philosopher, the waves were lapping against the beach. A gentle cold wind penetrated the Carhart coat sending a chill down Casey's spine. There were a few rugged souls bundled in winter coats and hats with their hands shoved into their pockets walking in the sand. They were leaning into the breeze, their scarves fluttering like sea gull feathers ruffled by the wind.

"What's your name?" Casey asked.

"Charles, Charles Franken."

"Not Charley?"

"No, not Charley. One of the denizens calls me Frankenstein half the time. My God his mind is burnt out!"

"My name is Casey."

"Nice to meet you Casey, but I'm thinking this is strange. You were deep in thought when I came upon you, and I thought something wasn't right, but now you're heading off to take up residency beneath a bridge. I'm getting some strange vibes. What about your car?"

"I won't need it. I'll call the rental company to pick it up."

Charles rubbed his chin, smoothing his wiry beard. "We could use a car to go get things," he said.

"Nah. I can't keep it. The cops are probably looking for that car right now. If they find it here, they might be able to track me down. It's best to get it back to the rental company."

"What did you do? Are you on the run?"

"Oh, thirty years ago, I robbed a museum. I've been hiding a bunch of valuable paintings in a ventilation pipe ever since. The FBI would like to get me in and sweat it out of me, where I stashed that stuff."

"That's interesting. Why did you do it"

Casey knew by Charles' tone that he didn't believe him. "I don't know why I did it, Charles. I don't know why I do anything," he said, smiling.

"You know you'll need blankets," Charles said.

"Me casa, su casa, didn't you say? I guess you don't have an extra blanket?"

"None you'd want to sleep under."

"I could go to a store. Is there anything around here?"

"The Target store is on the other side of Joe Moakley Park, but you'll have to carry everything you get. They're really stingy with their carts. They'll stop you if you try to leave the parking lot with a cart. I guess you have money?"

"I've got money. That's the least of my problems."

Charles walked with Casey across the park and into the Target store. The security guard watched them with interest as they tried to locate the home goods section. Just when they found the blankets and pillows the guard approached them. He looked at the bag Casey had slung over his shoulder. "What's in the bag?" He asked.

"Artwork."

"Mind if I take a look in that bag?"

"Not at all but be careful. These are my best paintings. They're individually wrapped in cellophane," Casey said. He unfurled the strap and placed the bag on the floor.

The guard unzipped the bag and pulled out the top three paintings. "We don't have anything like this in our store, so I guess you're alright," he said.

Casey took the paintings out of the guard's hands and placed them back in the bag. "Have a great day," he smirked. The guard shrugged, "Just doing my job. The sign at the entrance says we have a right to search all bags entering or leaving the store. Have a great day."

Casey nodded as he and Charles grabbed a pillow and two blankets.

After they left the store Charles said, "Are those the valuable paintings you stole?"

"Yep. There's a twelve-million-dollar reward for their return."

"I guess the jokes on him, then," Charles said.

"The jokes on him," Casey agreed.

"No reason to get excited, the thief, he kindly spoke, there are many here among us who feel that life is but a joke," Charles hummed.

"Socrates?"

"No, Bob Dylan again. Love Minus Zero."

They crossed Joe Moakley Park, walked north on the beach and crossed the street to the overpass on I-95. Bottles and plastic bags littered the ground and a half dozen grocery carts stuffed with blankets and filthy clothing were parked in various locations beneath the bridge. "That's all private property over there," Charles said, pointing to the carts. "You might get cut if you get near that stuff. Some of these guys are mentally ill."

"Got it," Casey said.

They approached a dirty mattress covered with a

blanket and a rock on each corner anchoring it down. Charles tipped up the side of the mattress and started digging through debris beneath it until he found a roll of foam padding. He handed it to Casey. "This is soft. You need to put one of your blankets on it and sleep beneath the other. That foam will absorb your body heat and keep you warm."

"Where'd you get the mattress?"

"Alongside the interstate. People pile their things on trucks like the Beverly Hill Billie's and things blow off. Finding a mattress on the interstate is as common as pigeon shit.

As Casey arranged the foam padding and blankets on the ground the burner phone rang. "Is that you, Mr. Brady?"

"Yes. We're ready to negotiate."

"There's no negotiation. You'll do as I say or the conversation is over," Casey said.

It was quiet on Brady's end.

"This is what I want, Mr. Brady. I want three John Doe blanket immunities signed by a federal judge, and a letter of intent signed by the Chief Circuit Judge of Suffolk County, Maryland. In addition, you must have the twelve million dollars divided in three equal shares, in three separate accounts ready for transfer to offshore numbered accounts that I will provide. In addition to that I've prepared an agreement that there will never be a civil action brought in this case. I'll text it to your number."

"How do we provide immunity to individuals when we don't have a name. Anyone could be John Doe, and by the same token, anyone could be denied immunity unless a name is provided," Brady said.

"Word the immunity petition that any and all participants in the robbery of the ISG Museum, and all parties in possessions of items obtained in the robbery and all parties having knowledge of the robbery are immune from prosecution. I think that will cover every aspect of the immunity order. Label them as John Doe 1, John Doe 2, and John Doe 3. You could almost use that exact terminology but if you want to word it differently, do so, but it must basically express the same terms."

"I agree with the statement, and I believe it will stand up in court, but there is the other matter at hand. How will the paintings be handed over?"

"Call me when the orders have been signed, and the accounts are ready for the transfer of money. I'll let you know how it will be done in a manner acceptable to all parties concerned. I won't be using this phone. I have a different cell where I can be reached." Casey said, and then he gave Brady the number of the new burner. When he hit the end button, he threw the phone into the concrete support of the underpass. It was shattered into pieces and fell among the other trash littering the ground.

Charles was watching Casey and listening to the conversation. There was an expression of wonder and disbelief plastered on his face. He waited a long time before he spoke. "I'm not really a PhD in philosophy," he said.

"I know," Casey said.

"But you really are a lawyer, and those paintings you're carrying around with you are really worth a fortune."

"Yep." Casey said.

"How do you know I won't hit you in the head with a rock and take'm?"

"I just know, Charles." Casey said. "You'll probably be sitting up during the night looking at me while I'm sleeping, thinking maybe you could take them and get a lot of money out of this deal. As the city gets darker, the rumbling traffic on I-95 above us goes silent, and the cold seeps into our blankets, you'll be sitting there wondering what it would be like to have all that money; but when morning comes, you'll still be sitting there, and the paintings will still be in that bag."

Charles sat down beside Casey. "You're an amazing man. You know things, don't you Casey," he said.

"I do, Charles. I know things."

Chapter Twenty-Two

As darkness descended, Casey was nestled in the bed he had prepared. A burn barrel was lighted, and several homeless men were sitting on the ground with the light flickering on their faces. Grungy beards and wiry hair were visible in an umber glow like Christ in Emmaus, by Rembrandt.

Casey pulled the blanket up tight against his chin, holding the burner to his ear. He called Mickey's and left the number of the burner with Helen, asking her to give it to Jason or Billy if they came in. He closed his eyes and went to sleep. At three am the foam padding had flattened out and hardened against the ground. Casey's muscles were aching. He turned slowly as his spine made a crackling sound. With one eye open he saw Charles sitting on a concrete block with his chin resting in his hand, staring at the duffle bag. Casey smiled and went back to sleep.

When the gray light of morning began to illuminate the Boston skyline, Casey rolled off his padding and stretched. Charles was sitting on his mattress. "I need to go back to the beach and take a shower and maybe hit that Target store for a toothbrush and shaving gear," Casey said. Charles gave Casey a curious glance. "You're not going to check the duffle bag?" he asked.

"Nope," Casey said.

Charles shrugged. "I'll tag along."

Casey flipped the duffle bag strap over his shoulder and headed for the beach. It was quiet and empty. Noise from traffic on I-95, and the normal city activity in the background seemed far away. Waves from high tide were beating against the sand. Gray clouds, and dark ocean water merged creating the impression that they were as one, stretching into infinity. Casey and Charles walked without speaking. When they reached Joe Moakley Park, Charles decided to sit while Casey went on alone. Casey made the trip to Target. He picked up soap, shaving cream, a razor and a towel. When he got back to the park Charles was still there. Casey studied Charles for a long moment. Charles looked back. "What?" He said.

"Do you want to have some fun today?"

Charles chuckled. "I have fun every day," he said facetiously.

"Seriously. We need to shower and make ourselves as presentable as possible. We're going on a mission," Casey said.

Charles got up, "I'm ready," he said. His beard was bristling, and long hair gnarled around the edges of his cap. Those strange steel gray eyes focused on Casey as his lips turned up in a faint smile. "Give me the details, Casey. I'm all in."

As they walked Casey laid out a plan. When they reached the beach showers, Charles was scratching his head. Another day in the life of Charles Franken, he thought.

After they were showered and Casey had shaved, Casey called for an Uber to pick them up at Joe Moakley Park. The driver seemed a little nervous about boarding them, but when Casey handed him a hundred-dollar bill, his tension was relieved. Casey asked the driver to take them to a reputable men's salon downtown. Fifteen minutes later they arrived at Di Salvos Barber Shop on Beacon Street. It was early so they were both seated immediately. When they sat down Charles looked like he was fifty years old. When the barber was finished, and dusting Charles' neck with talcum powder, he didn't look a day over thirty-five. Casey got a trim and his eyebrows were touched up. When it was all done Casey was relieved of another two hundred bucks. As the money was handed over Charles raised his eyebrows and gave Casey an inquisitive look. "I told you I have money," Casey said.

The Uber driver was still waiting when Casey and Charles finished at Di Salvos. Casey tipped him and told him to have a good day. They walked the mile from Di Salvos to Copley Square. Casey carried the duffle bag strapped across his shoulder. Five-hundred million just wasn't that heavy. Charles gazed at the buildings and streets as if he had never seen anything like it before.

When they entered the Nieman Marcus store they received a few curious glances before a salesman approached them. A sophisticated athletic black man. He was wearing an expensive suit with the cuffs above his ankles, exposing red hose. "Are you gentlemen looking for something?" He asked. His tone might have suggested, are you looking for the subway?

Casey got it. They didn't look like they could afford chicken wings from Colonel Sanders Kentucky Fried Chicken. Charles' clothes were clean, but ragged. Casey might have just come out of a blind duck. "I want a Giorgio Armani suit for each of us, and I want them tailored to fit," Casey said.

The salesman's eyes widened in surprise. "Sir, that

would be a purchase of about five-thousand dollars."

"About fifty-two hundred with the tip, right?"

The salesman's face brightened, and the corners of his lips turned up. "Right this way gentlemen," he said.

After they were fitted and the alterations complete, Charles examined himself in the mirror. He turned from one side to the other, arching his back in different poses. Casey sat on the leather couch watching him. Charles looked completely at ease in his twenty-five-hundred-dollar duds. When they walked out onto the street, they were both wearing Louis Vuitton shoes and bright red hose. There wasn't a man in downtown Boston or in a ritzy neighborhood like Beacon Hill who was better dressed. Casey called for an Uber, and they waited at the main entrance of Copley Place. Charles had both hands in his pockets. His lips stretched in a tight line. "You really are rich, aren't you, Casey?" He said.

"Yep."

"The lawyer business must be booming?"

"I never made more than a meager living lawyering. A junkyard owner left me more money than I could spend in a lifetime."

"So, you like to throw it around." Charles said, not questioning the absurdity of a junk man having that kind of money.

"I've been tight fisted until now, but it may be the last chance I have to extend some generosity," Casey said.

"Why are you messing with these valuable paintings if you have all the money you need? Why don't you just give them back?"

"I don't know, Charles."

When the Uber car arrived, it was the same driver they had before. He didn't have a clue they were the same men. He jumped out of the car and opened the door for them. "Good morning, gentlemen. Where am I taking you?"

Chapter Twenty-Three

FBI Agents, Ford and Green were in Lyle Hammonds office reviewing Casey's file. Hammond was anxious. He wanted to prosecute the ISGM heist like a fat kid wants cake. He was astounded by the information they had on Billy. He already knew Jake Brenner was shaky in more ways than one but finding an accomplice who was as simple minded as Billy was disturbing. Would a jury find it believable that an entourage like that could pull off the heist of the century?

"Maybe Jason Keys is the real leader of the gang who can't shoot straight," Hammond said.

"Green was shaking his head, completely in disagreement. Ford said, "No way. It's Rakestraw. He's had this thing hanging in the balance for thirty years, and he hasn't cracked. He's been questioned nine, maybe ten times by some pretty good agents. Until that scarecrow thing got the evidence tumbling along, we didn't have anything concrete. Now we do, and Dean Allen Marlo, and Leon Brady are trying to gum it up."

Hammond rubbed his chin. His forehead furrowed and the muscles in his jaw twitched. "I'm getting an arrest warrant for all three. You need to find Rakestraw. The other two should be sitting ducks."

As Ford and Green were leaving Hammonds office, Hammond said, "Let's get this guy. If we break this case, we're going places."

When they got on the elevator Green said, "Lee, let's get these guys, we're going places." Ford laughed. "I'm already where I wanna be, Ty."

When Casey and Charles got into the Uber, Casey didn't have a destination, so he said, "Just drive around." At that moment, the burner rang. It was Leon Brady. His legal team had finalized the paperwork Casey had demanded. The individual bank accounts were in place awaiting the information on the numbered offshore accounts. John Doe immunity documents were signed by Federal Judge Edwin Wilhelm, authorizing the Immunity Orders, and Letters of Intent by Suffolk County States Attorney Norman Black had been filed. Everything at that point was a go.

"Do we need to set up a location to access the authenticity of the paintings by examining the polaroid pictures?" Brady asked.

"How long will it take you to arrange for Marlo and the art specialist to be present?"

"They're both here now. We're ready at a moment's notice. In addition, I have another observer here who can guarantee that our agreement will stand up to scrutiny."

"Keep them there, I'll call you," Casey said, hitting the end button. He hesitated for a few seconds and then dialed the Virden police department number. When Casey asked for Jason, the dispatcher said he was on patrol, but she could patch him through. When Jason answered Casey said, "It's me."

"Casey, this phone is internet accessible. Anyone with a radio monitor from Walmart can listen in."

"It doesn't matter now. Just get Billy and grab the first flight you can get to Boston International. Call me on this phone when you get there. I need for the three of us to get together."

"Got it, Casey, but what's going on? Where have you been?"

"I slept under the I-95 overpass last night, but it's all good now."

The line was silent for a long time before Jason spoke. "Casey, I'm a little short on cash. A plane ticket is a little steep for me right now"

"Billy's got money, but if he doesn't, empty your bank account. Nothing matters more than you getting here," Casey said.

"Okay. I'll find Billy and catch a flight out of Springfield. I'll call when we get to Boston International."

As soon as Casey hung up. He dialed Leon Brady. "Have your team in your office at 3:00 tomorrow afternoon. I'll call you and give you a location for our meeting. We'll be ready on this end," he said, hitting the end button.

As Jason and Billy waited in the terminal not knowing where they were going or what fate awaited them, it left them time to think about their destiny. Billy had never been in an airplane in his life. The flight was akin to getting a surprise ticket to a carnival ride.

Billy watched passengers boarding and exiting as they sat on the hard vinal chairs, satisfied with examining his surroundings, but still there were questions swirling in his thoughts. Finally, staring out into the ether, he asked, "Jason, why did you do this? I mean rob the Ida, whatever her name is, Museum?

"Ida Swigert Graham Museum," Jason said.

"Yeah, what you said. Why did you do it?" They had

both been through this before, but here alone in a strange place, sitting at the edge of the unknown, it seemed an appropriate question to ask.

Jason looked at the floor for a long time before speaking. When he did, his voice was soft and low. "I wanted revenge. Dean Allen Marlo took away my life, Billy. I was a cop. I wasn't some small-town Barney Fife, taking orders from the day shift foreman at City Water Light and Power who was elected Mayor by a fifty-two-vote margin. I had a real job doing something I loved. He took everything away from me. Ripping off five hundred million doesn't even come close to squaring the deal with that son of a bitch. I wish I could have done more."

Billy looked at Jason as if it were the first time he had ever seen him. There was emotion in his eyes. Billy felt lucky at that moment that he was Billy, and not Jason.

"I did it because Casey asked me to." Billy said.

They were both quiet again as the roar of a jet rumbled into the distance. The Uber driver descended the elevator with a sign on his chest reading JASON/BILLY, sparing them from sinking lower into their sad conversation. Jason called Casey to let him know they were there.

It was a quick trip downtown. Casey was waiting in the Four Seasons lobby. Jason was dressed in jeans and a black hoody sweatshirt. Billy was wearing the clothes he had worn to work; a gray short sleeve shirt, black dockers, and a yellow tie that was four inches short. The concierge was standing at the reception desk talking to the clerk when they came in. When he saw them, he muttered, "Out of towners looking for a restroom, or they're lost," an air of superiority in his tone.

As he started towards them the lines between his eyebrows furrowed. Casey was watching him. A flush of irritation caused his face to feel warm. This guy probably doesn't have as much money as Billy has stashed away, he thought.

"Are you gentlemen lost?" He asked.

Casey cut between them. "Why do you ask," he said edgily.

"Just being helpful," the guy said.

"Yeah, right."

The man looked at Casey's tailored Armani suit and Louis Vuitton shoes. "Just being helpful," he said again. Casey glared at him. "These men are worth five-hundred-million dollars," he said. The guy stepped away. "Enjoy your stay. We're at your service here at Four Seasons."

Jason looked Casey up and down and then examined the extravagant corridor. Billy was as relaxed as a fat cat lying in the sun. "That's a nice suit, Casey," he said. Casey smiled. I've got one for each of you too," Casey said.

Jason was jittery. His face was strained with worry. "What's going on Casey? What's with the clothes and the five-star hotel?"

"We're leaving here as millionaires, or we're headed for prison. Either way, we're going in style," Casey said.

They took the elevator to the eighteenth floor. Jason and Billy each had their one-bedroom suite waiting for them. Billy's refrigerator was stocked with diet Coke, smokehouse sausages and Wyke Farms cheddar. A bottle of Kathryn Hall cabernet sauvignon was on ice in Jason's suite. Jason picked it up and read the label. Casey was still standing in the doorway watching him. Jason whistled and looked at Casey. "I'm no wine connoisseur, but I know this stuff is two-hundred dollars a bottle," he said.

"Two seventy-five here in the hotel," Casey said. Jason's mouth dropped open, but he didn't speak. He emitted a soft gasp and shook his head.

"I'm getting Billy. I'll grab a few beers and we'll be right back. I'm bringing a guest."

Jason turned his palms out. "Okay."

When Casey returned, Billy and Charles were following him. Billy was dressed in his Armani suit, but the cuffs were dragging on the floor. Jason watched Billy sliding his feet across the floor to avoid stepping on the cuffs. Charles was carrying a garment bag over his shoulder. "This is Charles, and that's your suit. A tailor will be up soon to do the alterations. In the meantime, let's have a beer or a glass of wine, or both," Casey said.

"I don't want to be rude, Casey, but who is this guy?" Jason said.

"This is Charles, I stayed at his place last night."

"I thought you stayed under the overpass on I-95?" Jason said.

"I did, Charles lives there."

A bewildered expression flushed onto Jason's face. "This is starting to get a little strange, Casey. What the fuck's going on!"

Just at that moment there was a knock at the door. "I'll get it," Casey said. He hurried to the door and found two men standing there. It was the tailer and a hair stylist. "While the tailer does the alterations, Billy can get a style and if you want you can get a trim," Casey said. Jason shrugged and turned his palms out. Billy dropped his pants to the floor and stepped out of them. The tailer took both Jason's and Billy's suits and stepped into an adjoining room. The hair stylist started working on Billy immediately, and the tailer worked with them separately to get measurements.

When everything was completed, the suits were hanging in the closet and Billy was sitting on the couch in his underwear and a t-shirt. Charles had helped himself to a glass of Kathryn Hall, Casey was having a Blue Moon, and Jason was staring at Casey with a mystified expression on his face. "Are we going to get the details, Casey, or are we going to party like there's no tomorrow?"

At that point Casey explained that he had been in contact with the ISG Museum lawyer. He laid out the details of the immunity deal, and the reward money that they had promised. If everything went right, they would be sitting pretty by the end of the next day. If not, they would be in Suffolk County Jail.

It took an hour for Casey to explain everything involved. When he was finished, they were quietly analyzing the situation.

"If we have immunity, why would they arrest us?" Jason asked.

"We're guilty of a criminal act. The FBI and federal prosecutors haven't been involved. They may want to prosecute the case under the grounds that the agreement was reached due to threat or ultimatum. A court may rule that the agreement was reached under duress. That would nullify the agreement. In that case Shaky Jake

Brenner would be the only one of us who would be safe from prosecution."

"That sucks," Billy said.

"Do you trust the museum lawyer?" Jason asked.

"No, lawyers can't be trusted.

Everyone was quiet again. Casey knew they were all thinking, why didn't we just leave things as they were? Reading the room, Casey said, "The feds were closing in on us. They forced my hand. We were going down if I didn't act. This could be the worst thing that could happen, but maybe the best. We'll know soon enough."

Jason picked up the Kathryn Hall and filled his glass. They all picked up a beer or took a glass of wine. Casey raised his Blue Moon. "Here's to tomorrow," he said.

At 2:00 pm the next afternoon, Brady and Marlo, along with an expert art examiner and four associates of Leon Brady were gathered in Brady's office waiting for Casey's call. They were prepared to go to whatever location Casey stipulated. It wouldn't take long before the other shoe would drop. All the immunity documents were signed and ready to go into effect, and the money had been deposited for transfer to the offshore accounts. Brady had a car waiting to take them and a security team prepared to follow. Marlo was eager to get the deal done. Twelve million dollars was chump change for him. The robbery and the longevity of the story were embarrassing. He just wanted it over with.

At that moment Casey and his group were checking out of the Four Seasons. When Casey presented the Gabby's Auto Salvage credit card the clerk tried to disguise her doubtful glance, but her expression was as if she had swallowed a fly. She was relieved when it went through without being denied.

The four of them standing in the lobby looked powerful. Casey examined them. They could have passed for a powerful law firm readying to close an historic settlement with General Motors on a wrongful death accident, or Phillip Morris for failing to disclose the harmful effects of nicotine. All that was missing was a camera crew following, waiting for the story to break.

When the credit card was activated, the FBI were immediately notified. Casey called for an uber car from the lobby. Within minutes after making the call the burner phone was identified and the location of the ping was transferred to FBI operations in Quantico, Virginia. Before the uber car arrived, Agents Ford and Green were already on the move, headed for downtown Boston.

Ford called Lyle Hammonds office to update him on the situation. "We've got a bead on Rakestraw," Ford said.

"Where?!"

"He's in Boston. We got a hit on his credit card at the Four Seasons Hotel."

"Are you sure it's him?"

"We got pings from a burner phone purchased in Milwaukee with a gift card. The first ping came in from the closest tower to the hotel."

"He's headed for Leon Brady' law office!" Hammond said.

"We'll keep you posted."

"I've got the warrants ready. I'll meet you there."

Green looked at Ford with raised eyebrows. "That's

not a good plan," he said.

Hammond's voice went up in volume, and urgency. "I'm in! I'm leaving my office right now," he said.

Casey purchased four Charles Simon handmade briefcases from the hotel gift shop for his crew to carry. When the uber arrived, the driver was quick to open the doors and assist them inside. Charles was carrying his briefcase and the duffle bag. The driver reached for the bag, but Charles pulled it away. He glanced at Casey with a little panic in his eyes. Casey shrugged. Charles let go and the driver tossed the bag into the luggage compartment.

Leon Brady, Dean Allen Marlo, an expert art examiner, and four of Brady' associate attorneys were gathered in the Brady executive office. Both Brady and Marlo had wondered aloud where the meeting place might take place. None of them knew what was happening with the FBI, or where Casey and his entourage were at the moment.

The uber driver dropped them at 160 Stuart Street where Brady law office occupied the entire twenty-first floor. When they approached the elevator, the people waiting parted like Moses parting the Red Sea. Charles Franken threw back his shoulders and straightened his suit as he stepped inside. When the elevator door closed Casey hit the express button. "Are we late," Jason asked.

"They don't know we're coming," Casey said.

Jason sighed, "Casey, you make me nervous."

"Whatever will be, will be," Casey said.

Billy looked at Jason. He put his thumb and forefinger to his lips and zipped them. Jason smiled. "I get it Billy."

When they entered the Brady Law Office, the receptionist was surprised. "Do you gentlemen have an appointment?"

"Tell Mr. Brady this is the call he's been waiting for. She typed in an email to the secretary in Brady's office. In a few moments Brady and two assistants were walking down the hallway. His expression was disbelief. "We were expecting a call," he said.

"I know, but that seemed a little inconsiderate. A visit between friends is always more appropriate, don't you think?" Casey said.

"Follow me," Brady snarled.

When they entered the office, Marlo looked stunned. "So, you're the firm representing the riffraff who robbed my museum?"

"We are," Casey said, looking directly into his eyes. He pitched the polaroid photographs onto Brady's desk. Brady nodded for the examiner to proceed. Time seemed to stand still as he hummed and hawed, inspecting the photos with a Loupes portable magnifier. After a long deep breath, he said, "They're the real thing."

Casey examined the immunity documents. "We need to transfer the reward money to these three offshore accounts," he said," handing a notepad to Brady. Brady handed the numbers to an assistant. "Get this done," he said.

"Bring the laptop in here. I want to see the transaction being made," Casey said. When the associate returned, he was being followed by an administrative assistant. They placed the computer on Brady's desk and the process was underway. Casey watched. Billy walked around to look over the associate's shoulder. His lip tightened, and he rubbed his chin as if in deep concentration. Confirmed, scrolled across the screen. Jason leaned over and whispered in Casey's ear. They have the numbers. Won't they be able to access the accounts?"

"That's a good question but I'll handle it," Casey said. He walked to a location behind Brady's desk. "Gentlemen, I'll save you some trouble. It's only natural for you to want to get into these accounts, but I've left instructions with the company handling them to provide extra security. This system is as secure as Fort Knox, so if you're thinking about fiddling with it, forget it."

Jason unconsciously shook his head in agreement.

"Now we need the paintings. We've done everything you asked," Marlow growled.

"Just one other thing, Mr. Marlow, I need a cashier's check made out to Charles Franken for Two hundred thousand dollars for legal services." Begrudgingly Brady sent one of the associates from the room to process the request. When he returned Marlo was steaming as Brady handed the check to Casey. "Mr. Franken, I hope you enjoy your two hundred grand. You'll never practice law again when I'm through with you!"

"You're probably right about that," Casey said. "In fact, I'm not Charles Franken. This is Charles," he said, pointing a finger at his newly acquired friend. "Charles is a philosopher. He has a place beneath the I-95 overpass near the Red Line."

Marlo's mouth dropped open.

"Give us a philosophical quote, Charles," Casey said.

"Revenge is sweet, but money is honey," Charles said.

"Bob Dylan?" Casey asked, smiling slightly.

No, that's Charles Franken right there."

Without warning, the office door banged open. A wild-eyed Lyle Hammond shouted." I have arrest warrants for these men!" Agents Ford and Green were behind him leading four other agents dressed in full combat gear. Casey reached into his coat pocket for the burner phone. Shouts from four different directions ordering him to drop the gun were instantaneous. Every agent in the room was aiming their nine millimeters at Casey's head. Casey held the phone up with his thumb and forefinger. He smiled at Marlo as he put the phone to his lips and said, "Burn the paintings."

Marlo jumped from his chair and ran to shield Casey from the agents. With both arms extended and hands out as if to catch the bullets, he shouted, "Everybody calm down. These men are attorneys!"

"We're taking them in," Hammond said.

Ford approached Casey and patted him down. The uniformed officers frisked the others. Ford looked at the battle-ready agents dressed in their black fatigues and body armor. "Stand down," he said. Marlo pointed towards the office door. "They need to go. Send them back to headquarters, or wherever it is they came from," he said. He glanced at Casey. "Resend your order to burn my paintings!"

"Stand by. Wait for my orders," he said, again pretending that there was a live person on the other end. "We need an exit strategy, or these paintings are going up in smoke," Casey said. Leon Brady addressed Hammond. "Mr. Hammond, leave the premises. We have all we need from the Justice Department.

"I'm not leaving, Leon. Whatever agreements have been signed were made under duress. The Supreme Court has ruled null and void contracts and agreements made under threat or duress."

At that moment Brady's cell phone pinged. Looking at the phone he said, "We have a visitor enroute from the lobby." While Brady was speaking the door opened and the US Attorney General Bertrand Steinbeck stepped in. "Lyle, it's over," he said without the slightest hesitation. Hammond gaped in surprise. "I've been in on these negotiations from the start. Mr. Marlo wants to pay the ransom. It's pocket change to him. He doesn't want the publicity. He doesn't want a trial, or even a news release. Now we need to clear the room and let them finish their business."

Hammond's face turned red and the tendons in his cheek were throbbing. "But!" he growled.

"No buts, unless you want a cubical in downtown Washington DC." Steinbeck said holding his hand up, palm out.

If the fire in Hammond's eyes could have transcended the room, the Attorney General's hair would have been scorched by his glare. He placed the warrants in his leather folder and slammed it shut. He looked at Agent Ford. "Politics wins," he said, nodding his head towards the exit. Green followed him but Ford walked over to Casey. "Excuse my language, but I'll just say this. You sonofabitch, you just might be DB Cooper after all." He smiled.

"Is that an insult or a complement?" Casey asked.

"A little of both."

"Well, you sonofabitch, thank you."

Charles Franken was staring at the cashier's check in his hand, wondering if this was real or a dream. Casey interrupted his thoughts. "Where's the bag?"

"I left it with the receptionist."

"Okay. Will you go get it?"

"Sure thing," he said, headed out to retrieve the bag. When he came back, he handed it to Casey. Casey placed it on Brady's Desk. "There you go," he said.

"What is it?"

"That's your paintings."

"What! They were in the lobby?" Marlo screeched.

"Yep."

Marlo rushed to open the duffle bag. He pulled out the paintings one by one. When he finished, he said to Brady, "They're all here."

It was finally over. There wasn't anything the law could do to them, and there was no reason to worry about being discovered. It felt liberating, and strange. "I guess we can go," Casey said. It was like a political debate. They were standing around, uncomfortable among those you had battled. Insults had been thrown around, attacking each other's integrity, and moral behavior but the fight was over, and the results were in. You were expected to be polite and civil. Is it time to shake hands and say good luck, Casey thought? Of course, it wasn't the same. Politics is a show. This was real life.

They shuffled slowly through the doorway and down the hall. When they got on the elevator Charles was still studying the check in his hand. "There's a party beneath the bridge under I-95 tonight. You're all invited," he said.

"You two have four million each," Casey said,

nodding to Jason and Billy.

"I don't need it," Billy said. " I want to keep my job?"

Casey laughed. "You can do whatever you want, Billy. You're rich."

"Three-way split, right?" Jason asked.

"Yep."

"I'll bet old shaky Jake Brenner pisses his pants when he hears about this," Billy said as the elevator door closed.

Chapter Twenty-Four

Jason and Billy decided to see the sights in Boston, and Charles returned to the overpass to throw a hell of a party, catered by Bay's Catering, one of the city's premiere food services. Casey rented a car and headed west on I-80. It took fourteen hours to get to I-39 at Lasalle, Illinois. He cut across country arriving in Kewanee an hour and a half later. It was seven o'clock in the morning. He was still wearing his Armani suit and Louis Vuitton shoes. He stopped at the Walmart and bought a few long sleeve T-shirts, a pair of jeans, and Nike loafers. By eight a m, he was in bed at the Motel Six on South Main Street. It was his intention to sleep all day, but he was restless. The museum heist had been a thorn in his side for thirty years, but now there was an unexplainable sense of loss. There was a hole in him big enough to drive a truck.

Jake Brenner was less than five blocks away. Casey wanted to confront Jake and bring this thing to its conclusion. Was it closure he was wanting? Trying to sleep was futile so he dressed in his casual clothes and packed the Armani suit and Louis Vuitton shoes in a guest garment bag from the closet. When finished, he checked out. There was a mist in the air and a light breeze sent a cold chill down his spine. Jake's antique store was straight up the street from the hotel, so it was only moments before Casey was standing in the doorway of the store. He could see Jake sitting behind the counter with a fixed expression on his face, staring off into nowhere. When Casey stepped inside, Jake didn't look up. "Welcome," he said in a feeble, tired voice. The smell of old things permeated the air. Old things like weathered leather, wool clothing that had been packed away for years, dust, and oily metal. Jake looked old. His hair was thin and gray. His receding hairline exposed age spots on his forehead.

We're all old. We've lived an entire lifetime with this hanging over our heads. He's as much a victim as Jason Keys, Casey thought. Casey quietly approached the counter and called Jake's name. Jake was so startled that he may have come out of his shoes. He dawdled to his feet and turned around as quickly as he could. It was a second before he recognized his partner in crime. His shock turned into fear as he snorted and giggled.

"Casey! It's you!"

"It's me Jake," Casey said calmly.

"Casey, don't kill me."

"Stop it, Jake. I'm not gonna kill you."

"What do you want, then. You know I ratted you out." His eyes met Casey's, and a sad pitiful expression materialized on his face.

Casey exhaled softly. "Jake, I'm gonna make this short and sweet. Our ordeal is over. I made a deal with the Feds and received a reward for returning the paintings. The charges have all been recalled and we all have immunity. That would include you. They gave us twelve million dollars. I gave Jason and Billy four million each, so they're off to Never, Never Land."

"That's their names, Jason and Billy?"

"Yes."

That's fair, Casey. I don't deserve anything. I'm a coward. I betrayed you."

"Jake, we'll probably never see each other again, so this is goodbye," Casey said. He extended his hand. Jake's fingers were trembling as he reached out to shake Casey's hand. Instead of shaking, Casey handed him a folded carbon card with gold imprint.

"What is this?" Jake asked.

"It's your share. That's a private account in the Cayman Islands, and the security code to access it."

"Casey, my God! It's four million dollars!"

"Yep."

"But you said…." Jake stuttered. "Four million three ways is twelve million. What about you, Casey?"

As Casey was walking out the door he said, "Don't worry about me, Jake. Have a good life."

Chapter Twenty-five

Two days later Casey was in Maple Creek, Oklahoma, driving down County Road Z. He remembered it being hilly and narrow, but now in the dark, the sun still hidden beyond the horizon, it was like being on a narrow pathway in a blackened forest. Each mile seemed longer than the last. When he finally reached Savanah's farm, the house was dark. He could see fresh new grass in the yard and daffodils in full bloom along the picket fence.

He stopped in the gravel driveway and reached into the back seat of his car to retrieve the garment bag with the Armani suit, and Louis Vuitton shoes. The morning sunlight was striking the top of the trees as a rooster was crowing in the barnyard. Casey slung the bag over his shoulder and walked out into the garden. He placed the shoes on the ground beneath the scarecrow and filled them with dirt. He placed a stick into each of them and wrapped them with cornstalk leaves, creating a pair of legs. He slipped the pants over them and filled them with straw. Casey used the belt to synch the pants tight against the scarecrow's waistline. He placed the Armani suit coat across the shoulder. He reached into his pocket and took out the stocking cap Charles Franken had given him when they were sleeping beneath the I-95 overpass. He placed it on Freddy's head, keeping it above the eyeline where Savanah had painted features. He stepped back to examine his work when the sun crested the tree line it lit up Freddy's face.

You can't see someone smiling when they are behind you, but sometimes you can feel it. When Casey turned, Savanah was standing on the porch. The oblique sunshine was radiating in her hair. "Freddy must have been a good boy to be lavished with such exquisite duds," she said.

"We're celebrating," Casey said. "Dean Allen Marlo has been reunited with his long-lost irreplaceable paintings, and I helped get them to him."

"I heard on the news that a concerned art investor purchased the paintings on the black market and returned them out of the goodness of his heart," Savanah said.

"It was supposed to stay under wraps. I guess it would be hard to keep a story like that from coming out," Casey said. "At least they came up with a believable spin."

"The FBI Bureau Chief said the case was still open and they would keep looking for the perpetrators until they were brought to justice."

"Well, yeah," Casey said.

Savanah was quiet for a long time before she spoke. She scrutinized the scarecrow with the twenty-five-hundred-dollar suit. "Let's let Freddy show off his new clothes. It's early. I'm going back to bed. Are you coming?"

"If I come in, I'm never leaving again."

"That's the plan," Savanah said.

The End